* * * * * * *

The stagecoach was making good time as it moved swiftly along the road. Once it was in the Dakota Territory, it would not be long before the stagecoach would have to slow down in the hills and valleys leading to its destination.

Up ahead was a portion of the road that was rather narrow and very crooked. It was well known as the most dangerous part of the trip, not only because of the crooked narrow road, but because the stagecoach had been robbed several times in the area.

* * * * * * *

FRONTIER JUSTICE

by

J.E. Terrall

ISBN: 978-0-9963951-8-2

This is a work of fiction. Names, characters, and incidents are either a product of the author's imagination or are used fictitiously, and any resemblance to actual persons, living or dead, is purely coincidental.

Printed in the United States of America
First printing / 2017 – Creatspace.com
Second printing; large print 2017 Createspace. com

Cover: Front and back cover photos taken by author, J.E Terrall. Photo of author taken by Phyllis Terrall

Book Layout/
Formatting: J.E. Terrall
           Custer, South Dakota

FRONTIER JUSTICE

To
Robert Campbell, my brother-in-law,
with best wishes.
I couldn't ask for a
better brother-in-law.

FRONTIER JUSTICE

THE LAWYER

I'd been slowly wandering across the vast prairie of the Dakota Territory for what seemed like forever. My horse and pack horse had been my only companions since I crossed the Missouri River almost four weeks ago. In fact, I had not seen another human being for the better part of the last three weeks.

The weather had been fairly hot and dry. I was hoping to find a settlement somewhere along the way, but hadn't seen one so far. Taking a minute or so to look around, I noticed a couple of trees off to the northwest. It had been my experience that where there were trees out on the prairie, there was usually water, and I was short on water.

I turned north and kept the trees in sight as I rode toward them. It wasn't long before I found a shallow stream. It was typical of most of the small streams I had seen on the prairie, wide but not very deep. The few trees along the bank of the stream were cottonwood trees.

I quickly decided it was a good place to spend the night and give my horses a chance to graze on the grass along the bank and to rest in the shade of the trees.

After taking my meager supplies off the pack horse and the saddle off my riding horse, I took the horses down to the stream for a good long drink of water. Since I was in need of water, too, I laid down on the bank of the stream and took a drink.

While I was lying down on the bank of the stream enjoying a drink of the clear, cool water, something floated by on the other side of the stream. I sat up and was surprised to see a block of wood with a small paper sail attached to it. It was a child's homemade boat.

I jumped up, splashed across the stream and chased it downstream until I caught it. Holding it in my hands, I just looked at it. Since it was in very good shape, I began to think it had not been in the water very long. Still standing in the stream, I looked up the stream in the direction it had come. Since it was a child's toy, there must be a settlement or, at the very least, a farm or ranch upstream.

I waded out of the stream taking the boat with me. Setting it down next to the tree, I set up my camp under the cottonwood trees. After building a fire and cooking the last of my salt pork, I made a pot of coffee, then leaned back against the tree to eat. While I ate, I decided that in the morning I would follow the stream north in the hope of finding a place where I might be able to get some supplies.

I set the boat aside then laid down on my bedroll. The night was warm and I could hear the sound of the leaves rustling in the trees as a gentle breeze drifted across the open prairie. It was a sound I had come to know, and it felt good to know that all was as it should be. I soon drifted off to sleep.

I woke just as the sun was coming up over the horizon. I got up and took the horses to the stream for a drink. When they were done, I tied them to one of the trees and let them graze on the grass at the base of the trees while I had my breakfast of biscuits and honey. The honey tasted good and caused me to remember that I got the honey from the wife of a farmer about three weeks back. When I was finished eating, I packed up.

After putting out the fire, I put what was left of my supplies on the pack horse along with the boat, then saddled my riding horse. I took a quick look around to make sure I had not left anything behind and had put out the fire. Sure that the fire was completely out and I had not left anything behind, I stepped up into the saddle and began riding north along the bank of the stream.

It wasn't very long before I could see a small group of buildings off in the distance. I smiled to myself thinking that I was finally going to see some people and get some supplies. The closer I got to the town, the more I could see of it. I had no idea what was going on, but there seemed to be a dozen or more people standing in the center of the street. There must be some sort of celebration going on in the town was my first thought. The closer I got to town, the more I was beginning to think it was not a celebration at all.

As I rode into town, I could see that there was a man standing in the center of the crowd, and he looked scared to death. Those in the crowd were yelling at the man, and I could see there were two men holding him. The man they were holding had his hands tied behind his back.

I stepped out of the saddle and tied my horse to a nearby hitching rail, then leaned back against the hitching rail to watch and listen. I wanted to see what was going on.

"I know he was the one who stole my cattle," a big man said with a harsh voice.

The big man looked like he was pretty well off. That thought was based on the clothes he wore. He had on a brown suit with a matching vest and a gold watch chain across his more than ample belly. The big man was obviously mad as hell as he waved his pointed finger at the man he was accusing of stealing his cattle.

From what I could see, it didn't look like the accused had a single friend in the crowd. That was until a small woman wearing an apron over a simple cotton dress stood up for the accused.

"I tell you, he could not have stolen your cattle. He was nowhere near your place," the small woman said angrily.

"You're his friend. You'd say anything to save his neck. He stole my cattle and is probably responsible for several other cattle that are missing," the well-dressed man said.

"I've had a few of my cattle stolen, too," another man yelled out.

"Me, too," a third man said.

"I say we string him up," someone I couldn't see yelled.

I watched the people in the crowd. It seemed the man accused of stealing cattle only had one person on his side, and it was the small woman.

There was a lot of yelling among the men in the crowd, but nothing was getting resolved. It was clear to me that it was slowly, but surely, turning into a lynch mob. All reason was gone. It had reached the point where no one was listening and the crowd was pushing in closer to the accused. I wondered where the law was, or if there was any law in this town.

Suddenly someone showed up with a rope. It didn't look good for the man accused of stealing cattle. I had never seen a hanging before, and I was in no hurry to see one now.

Something had to be done to quiet things down and give people a chance to think about what they were about to do.

I saw a couple of the men grab the accused and slip the rope over the accused's head and around his neck. I had to do something to stop it, and I had to do it now. I drew my gun from my holster and fired a shot into the air. The sudden sound of a gun going off stopped everything. At first, they all looked confused, but I soon had them all looking at me.

"Just a minute there," I yelled to get their attention.

I could see in their faces they wondered who I was and what I had to do with any of it. No one spoke for almost a minute.

"Who the hell are you?" the big man finally asked.

"I'm Albert Jones. You're taking the law into your hands, and that is not right," I said as I began to think I might be in trouble myself for interfering.

"This ain't none of your business. Butt out," the big man said.

"Every man is entitled to a fair trial. He should be turned over to the law."

"We are the law here," someone yelled. "I think you best get out of here 'fore we string you up alongside him."

"I'll shoot the first man that tries to hang him," I said with far more confidence than I was feeling at the moment.

I held my gun firmly in my hand and had it pointed right at the big man, the one who was so intent on hanging the accused. I was a bit nervous and was beginning to think I might have gotten into something that was more than I could handle. I was greatly outnumbered.

"No man should take another man's life without giving him a chance to defend himself," I said to the big man. "You have accused him of stealing your cattle. I also heard someone else express the idea that he stole his cattle, too. I also heard someone say he couldn't have done what you accused him of because he was some place else. You have to prove he did it."

I went on to say, "You can't hang a man based on hearsay, or because you don't happen to like him. If you hang him without a fair trial, you are guilty of murder. In fact, every one of you who assists in the hanging of this man in anyway, is also guilty of murder. And for those of you who don't do anything to stop it, are guilty of complicity."

I noticed that several of the people in the crowd had no idea what I said. I thought it would be a good idea to tell them what "complicity" meant.

"Complicity means you did nothing to stop it and may have encouraged those who carried out the hanging."

"What are you? Some kind of lawman?" a little man asked.

"Actually, I am some sort of a lawman. I'm an attorney, a lawyer."

"Then you know somethin' about the law, right?" the little man asked.

"I know a lot about the law. If you hang him, I will report all of you to the territorial marshal. He will come here with some deputies and arrest all of those who hung this man. He will charge everyone involved with murder."

Those in the crowd began to talk among themselves. From what I could hear, they weren't too sure I could do what I said, or that what I was telling them was true. Suddenly one of the men quieted the crowd down, then turned to me.

"If what you say is so, - -." he started to say when I interrupted him.

"What I said IS so."

"Okay. If you're a lawyer, then what do we do with him?"

"You have a choice. You can let him go and leave him be, or you can lock him up until a lawman can investigate your claim that he did what you have accused him of doing. If the lawman finds enough evidence to warrant a trial, then a circuit judge would come and have a trial."

"What if the judge finds him not guilty?"

"He would be set free, and that would end it."

"But we know he's guilty," one of the men in the crowd said sharply.

"Then prove it. But prove it to a judge."

"I say we hang him now," the big man demanded.

"You do and I'll see you hang next," I said looking the big man right in the eyes.

The big man just looked at me. From the look in his eyes I could see he hated me. I had upset his plans and he didn't like it. I'm sure he didn't like my gun pointed at him, either. There was a long silence before anyone spoke.

"You said we have to lock him up until a lawman can investigate. Where do we lock him up? We ain't got a jail," one of the town's folks said with a bit of laughter in his voice.

"I guess that's your problem," I said.

"And when is the territorial marshal going to come? I ain't never seen him around here," a scruffy looking man said.

"You said until a lawman can investigate, right?" a tall young man asked.

"Yes, I did."

"You're a lawman. You even said you was. You can investigate Mr. Simon's claim that he stole Mr. Simon's cattle," the scruffy looking man said.

"Yeah," was the reply from several in the crowd.

"I think that's a good idea," the small woman said. "He has no interest in this. He would be fair."

"Yeah," a number of those in the crowd agreed.

I thought about what had just happened. I wasn't sure how I got myself into this situation, but I apparently had. It reminded me of the saying 'no good deed goes unpunished'. With a man's life at stake, I felt I had to do it. I really had no choice if I truly believed what I was saying.

"Okay, I'll investigate, but I don't want anyone interfering with my investigation. If anyone interferes, I will charge them with obstruction of a lawful investigation. I also want the cooperation of the people in this community."

"You got it," a tall slim man said with a hint of confidence in his voice.

It was followed by several others agreeing. I must admit there were a couple of them who agreed reluctantly.

"First of all, I need a place to keep the prisoner. Some place where he can stay while I investigate Mr. Simon's claim of cattle rustling."

"I got a tack room in back of my livery stable you could use. I'll empty it out," the local blacksmith said. "I can put a bed in it."

"I can be like a deputy and keep an eye on him so he don't run off. It would give you time to do your investigation, too," a young man said.

"Okay. What's your name?"

"Bill Forth," the young man said.

"Okay, you are my deputy. It is your job to guard him and protect him."

"I don't like it one bit," Mr. Simon said. "He's going to let him go as soon as we turn our backs."

"I will not let him go, and I will investigate your accusations. I might add, I will arrest you and anyone else, and jail you, if you cause me any trouble or try to injure or kill my prisoner. You understand that?" I said looking right at Mr. Simon.

"Yeah, I understand," Mr. Simon agreed, but it was clear that he didn't like it.

Mr. Simon glanced at me then at the prisoner. He looked over the crowd, too, before he stormed off. As he walked away, I wondered why he was in such a hurry to hang this man. I could think about that later. Right now, I had to get my prisoner locked up and get myself settled in.

"Bill, take our prisoner over to the livery stable. As soon as the blacksmith - - - - ."

"Mr. McDougal," Bill offered quickly.

"As soon as Mr. McDougal gets the tack room cleaned out and a bed put in it, lock the prisoner up."

"Yes, sir," Bill said.

I watched Bill take our prisoner down the street to the livery stable. Mr. McDougal walked alongside Bill. I turned and walked over to where I had left my horses. As I reached out to untie my horse, a small boy was looking at my pack horse. I looked at him for a moment.

"Can I help you, son?"

"Can I have my boat back, mister?" he asked softly.

"Sure thing," I said as I took the boat off my pack horse. "It made it almost five miles down the river from here and was still going when I caught it."

"Wow. Thanks, mister," he said then ran down the street with his toy boat.

I untied my horses and swung into the saddle. I couldn't help but think about that toy boat. It was the reason I was here.

"You ain't leavin' are ya?" the small man said.

"No, I'm not leaving. I'm taking my horses to the livery stable. By the way, what's your name?"

"I'm Freddy Small. I work at the saloon."

"Freddy, I would like you to listen in on any conversations that Mr. Simon might have in the saloon and report back to me. You think you can do that?"

"Sure. You think he's up to something?"

"He seemed very disappointed he wasn't going to be able to hang, ah. Say, what's the name of the guy he wanted to hang?"

"That was Josh Timmer."

"What does he do around here?"

"He owns a small ranch out north of town. It borders on Mr. Simon's ranch. Josh and Mr. Simon have had a running feud for several years."

"What about?"

"I'm not sure, but I think it's about land. Simon wants the land Josh has, and Josh don't want to give it up."

"Why does he want Timmer's land?"

"'Cause he's got water all year 'round, while the creek that flows through Simon's land usually dries up by mid-August."

"Thanks," I said.

I swung my horse around and headed for the stable with my pack horse in tow. As I rode toward the stable, I thought about Simon and the feud he was having with Josh. It looked to me like I had found one person who had a reason to want Josh dead. I wondered if there might be others who had it in for Josh. If so, who and why?

When I arrived at the livery stable, Mr. McDougal was standing at the door. I reined up and stepped out of the saddle.

"I got the tack room fixed up so you can keep your prisoner in it. It ain't got no windows."

"I guess that will have to do. We'll have to let him out from time to time to relieve himself. During the day when Bill's here, he can be outside, but he'll have to be restrained."

"I got some shackles you can use. You can put them on him when he's outside. I can fix 'um so you can chain him to a post inside or out. He'd be able to move around a bit, but he wouldn't be able to escape."

"That would work. I want to have a talk with Josh."

"You want him in shackles before we let him out?" McDougal asked.

"No. I don't think that will be necessary. Are you and Bill going to be here?"

"Yeah."

"Okay, bring him out. I want the two of you to be close by."

McDougal nodded that he understood, then turned and went into the barn. It didn't take but a minute for Bill and McDougal to return with the prisoner. I pointed to a bale of hay for Josh to sit on. As soon as he was seated, I sat down on another bale of hay.

"Josh, I want you to tell me everything that happened from the time you got up this morning to when I came here."

"You think it's going to do any good," he said sharply. "Simon has all the money and all the people here under his thumb."

"He doesn't have me under his thumb. Just tell me what I asked."

"Okay. I got up this morning and went out to take care of my horse. In the corral, I found several cattle with Simon's brand on them."

"How did the cattle get in your corral?"

"I have no idea, but their tracks showed that they had come from Simon's ranch, and had probably been driven into my corral."

"What did you do then?"

"I started to run them back to Simon's ranch when he came riding out of a ravine not far from my corral. He had several of his men with him. I couldn't swear to it, but I think they had been waiting in the ravine until I started to move the cattle out of the corral.

"I think Simon would have killed me right there except he would not like so many witnesses if he killed me right on the spot. They brought me into town and almost immediately began getting everyone all riled up. He even had a couple of other ranchers say they had cattle stolen by me. I don't know if they had cattle stolen or not, but I do know they are in hock up to their necks to Simon. I guess they were just looking for someone to blame for the missing cattle, if there were any cattle that were really missing," Josh said.

"I understand you have been having a running feud with Simon. What was that all about?"

"It's kind of a long story."

"I've got time, and so do you."

"I'll make it brief, but you'll get the idea. Simon was in love with Martha Coleman, a young girl who was very pretty. She didn't want anything to do with Simon. He tried almost everything he could think of to get her to marry him, but nothing turned her head toward him.

"Martha set her sights on me. That made Simon very angry. The funny thing was, she was actually in love with a young man who lived with his folks on a ranch south of here. Shortly after they were married, they left the area. I heard they went to California, but no one seems to know where they went for sure, and no one has seen them again. Simon blamed me for her running off and marrying the young man."

"That is a little strange," I said.

"Maybe, but it's true. After she left, he started trying to get me to leave the country. As the years passed, he got more and more angry. He sent one of his men over to beat me up in order to get me to leave, but the guy ended up getting his head cracked open and left the country without returning to Simon's ranch. He even hired a man to kill me, but as you can see he didn't get the job done. I killed his hired gunman when he missed me with the first shot. The problem was I couldn't prove he had sent either one of them to run me off or kill me."

"That's quite a story."

"I always thought that Mr. Simon was not right in the head. He sure wasn't right in the head after Martha left. I think he thought I got Martha to marry the young man and leave, but I had nothing to do with it."

"Did you love Martha?"

"No, and she didn't love me. We were just friends."

"I heard it was due to a lack of water that Simon wants your ranch; you have it all year round, and he doesn't."

"That's not true. He has a river that runs across the northern end of his ranch. It has water in it all year round. He has plenty of water for his cattle."

"Where is your ranch from here?"

"It's about three miles straight north of here. You can't miss it. There's a small cabin and a barn straight west of the cabin. There's a stream that runs just about ten feet behind the cabin. Bill can show you where it is," Josh said.

"I'm going out there in the morning. I want to take a look around. You just sit tight."

"I don't have much choice."

I just nodded then left Josh to be locked up while I went to the only boarding house in town. I checked in and noticed that the woman running the place was the small woman who had stood up for Josh.

Good evening, Mr. Jones. I'm Betty Shaw. Dinner will be ready soon. I have a room for you on the second floor. It's room three. You can put your things in the room and come back down for dinner."

"Thank you, Miss Shaw."

"It's Mrs. Shaw. My husband died four years ago, and left me this boarding house."

"I'm sorry. What do I owe you for a couple of nights?"

"There's no charge since you're helping Josh, I mean Mr. Timmer."

"Thank you."

I got the feeling she was a little more interested in Josh than she was in justice. From the look on her face, she might be a little sweet on him. I wondered if the feeling might be shared.

"Breakfast will be at six," she said as I started for the stairs to the second floor.

I turned and smiled to let her know I had heard her, then went up the stairs. I found room three was located at the front of the house and overlooked the street. Looking out the window I could see the blacksmith's shop and livery stable clearly.

I put my things away, then went downstairs to dinner. It was a very good meal. After dinner, I went to my room. It was a warm night and I had a lot on my mind. I sat in the window and looked out at the livery stable. I wasn't really looking at anything, just thinking about the man locked up in the livery stable.

My attention was taken away from my thoughts when I heard a knock on my door. I picked up my gun and went to the door.

"Who is it?"

"It's me, Freddy Small."

I opened the door, looked around then let him in.

"What is it?" I said as I closed the door behind him.

"You said for me to keep my ears open in the saloon."

"Yes, I did. Did you hear something?"

"I sure did. Mr. Simon was sittin' at a table off in the corner with two of his men. They was talkin' quiet like, but I could hear 'um. They was talkin' about breakin' Josh out of the tack room, then killin' him once they got him away from town."

"Did they say when they were going to break him out?"

"As soon as it gets quiet and shortly after the light in your room goes out."

"Find Bill and tell him to take cover behind that wood box next to the general store."

"You goin' to ambush 'um?"

"I'm going to take them alive if we can, but I don't want anyone to risk their life to get them alive. I'll do what I have to do to stop them from killing Josh, if I can."

"Yes, sir."

I watched as Freddy left my room. I got my gun and strapped it on. As soon as I was ready, I sat down next to the window, but not where I would be an easy target, or where someone outside might see me. Looking out the window, I waited and watched.

It had grown dark making it hard to see anyone that might be hiding between the buildings. The only light on the street was the light coming from the saloon. With the saloon on the same side of the street as the boarding house, I could not see who was going in or out.

I'm not sure how long I waited next to the window, but it was getting pretty late. The noise from the saloon had died down to almost nothing. As I glanced out at the space between two of the buildings on the other side of the street, I saw a light come on, then quickly go out. After that I could only see the glow of a cigarette. There was someone between the buildings. It was time to make my move.

I moved over to the table next to the bed and blew out the lamp. With the room dark, I left the room and went down the stairs and out the back of the boarding house. I didn't know if Freddy had found Bill or not, but it was time to catch them trying to get Josh out of the tack room.

I worked my way down along the back of the boarding house to the back of the saloon. I opened the backdoor and quietly snuck into the saloon's back room. Standing next to the door, I could hear Mr. Simon. It was easy to pick out his voice.

"How long has his light been out?" I heard Simon ask, but couldn't see who he was talking to.

"About thirty minutes."

"Okay. Let's go get Josh. Try not to kill him here. I want it to look like he escaped and got away."

I then heard what sounded like three men walking across the wood floor of the saloon and out the front. I quickly left the saloon by the backdoor. Running as fast as I could without making too much noise. I moved behind the buildings until I was just across the street from the front of the livery stable. I waited.

If Bill was where he was supposed to be, we would have them in a crossfire. It wasn't but a minute or so when I saw three men walking next to the boardwalk on the other side of the street. They were walking toward the livery stable. Two of the men kept looking around as if they expected trouble. The third man was Simon. He was strutting along as if he owned the town.

"That's far enough," I called out.

I didn't have time to say anything else. They quickly drew their guns and began firing in my direction as they tried to take cover. I kept my head down, but I could hear return fire. It was the return fire that got them shooting at the others. I saw one of them running toward the livery stable. I took aim, fired, and hit him in the leg. He fell in the street.

A shot from somewhere took a chunk of wood out of the corner of the general store near my head. I felt a piece of it hit me. It only stung a bit, but I didn't have time to worry about it. I returned fire and another man dropped out of the darkness into the light from a building across the street. Since I heard another shot at the same time I fired, I wasn't sure if I hit him or not.

"Hold it right there," I heard Bill call out.

There were two shots fired almost at the same time, then it was quiet. I waited and listened, but heard nothing for at least a couple of minutes.

"It's all over, Mr. Jones," Bill said.

I took a deep breath then stepped out of the shadows just as Bill stepped out of the darkness across the street. I could see three men. One in front of the livery stable clutching his knee. It was obvious he was in a great deal of pain. Two other men were lying dead, one in the street and one on the boardwalk. The dead one in the street was Simon.

"Bill, take care of them. I'm going to let Josh Timmer loose."

"Yes, sir."

I turned and went inside the livery stable. I took the key off the peg near the door, unlocked the lock and opened the door. I could see Josh sitting on the bed. The lamp next to the bed shined on his face. The expression on his face was that of a man who felt suddenly relieved.

"What was all the shooting about?"

"It seems Mr. Simon wanted you dead, but things didn't turn out that way. You are free to go. He will not bother you again. He's dead."

Josh walked out of the tack room and out onto the street in front of the livery stable. He was greeted by Bill and Freddy who immediately told him what had happened.

I returned to the boarding house and was met by Betty. I could see the concerned look on her face.

"It's all over. Josh is fine, and he is free. Simon will no longer be a problem," I said.

"Thank you so much," Betty said just as Josh came in the door.

I watched as Betty ran to Josh and threw her arms around his neck. She kissed him. I smiled, then turned and went upstairs to my room. I went straight to bed.

The next morning, I packed my belongings and went downstairs to breakfast. I was joined for breakfast by Bill, Freddy, and Josh.

Betty served us a very good breakfast. It seemed that most of the time was spent with them trying to get me to stay in their little town, but I gracefully declined the offer. After declining several times, they finally gave up and wished me a safe journey.

I added fresh supplies to my pack horse, saddled my riding horse then swung into the saddle. I waved to my new-found friends as I rode out of town and headed west.

A NEED TO RUN

A large buckskin horse plodded along in the darkness as it moved slowly across the grasslands of the Dakota Territory. There was only a sliver of a moon occasionally peeking out between the clouds as they floated across the night sky. A soft breeze drifted across the vast open prairie. A rider was hunched over the neck of the horse as it continued to move westward. The rider was Gill Beamon.

Gill Beamon was a bounty hunter. For the past several weeks he had been dogging the Saxtons. The Saxtons had left a trail of death and destruction across the southern part of the Dakota Territory. They had stolen what they needed from ranches and farms over an area almost a hundred miles long. As far as Gill knew, they had left four men dead, and burned down several barns and ranch houses along the way.

Gill had tracked them into an area of the territory that was filled with gullies, deep ravines and some heavily wooded areas along the Missouri River. It was in that area where he lost them. He spent several days trying to pick up their trail but without success.

He was about to head back in an effort to pick up the Saxtons' trail again when he felt a sharp pain in his leg that was immediately followed by the sound of a rifle shot. It was suddenly clear they had found out that Gill was trailing them, and they had managed to circle around behind him.

Gill kicked his horse and took off as fast as his horse could go. He ran his horse in and around the trees, and in and out of the ravines, finally losing the Saxtons as darkness started to spread over the land. He didn't quit. Gill continued out into the grasslands, only allowing his horse to slow down when he was sure he had lost them. Although he had slowed down, he kept his horse moving.

As he continued west, his thoughts turned to how the Saxtons had found out he was trailing them. The only thing he could think of was that someone had told the Saxtons he was looking for them. Gill had been trailing them for a long time and thought he was getting closer. During that time, he had come across a few small ranches. He would ask for information on the whereabouts of the Saxtons. One or more of the ranchers must have told the Saxtons about Gill looking for them.

However, the Saxtons attempt at bushwhacking Gill had done nothing to get the results they wanted. Gill had managed to escape even though he was injured. The Saxtons knew he would have to find a place to holdup to take care of his wound. They also knew what kind of a bounty hunter Gill was. He was the kind that would not give up in the pursuit of a criminal. They also knew he brought in more of the men he hunted dead than alive.

The Saxtons decided to turn the table on him and hunt him down. They went back to where they had last seen his trail. With the darkness, it would be hard to follow him. They decided to wait until morning to pursue him and kill him.

Once Gill had shaken the Saxtons, he was out on the prairie. Gill also knew he had left a trail that would not be hard for a good tracker to follow. In an attempt to gain greater distance and time, he rode all day and all night. He only stopped for a few brief times to let his horse graze and get a drink of water from streams and creeks he happened to come upon.

Gill had pushed hard across the prairie for three days and three nights. In the darkness of the third night, Gill's weary horse stepped into a shallow creek. Up to then Gill had managed to stay on the horse, but Gill's weight shifted in the saddle when the horse stepped into the creek. He tried to keep from falling, but he was too tired and weak. He slid off the horse and fell into the shallow creek.

Falling into the cold water surprised Gill at first, but the cool water felt good on his injured leg. He knew that riding so far, and for so long, had inflamed his wound. He sat up in the creek and looked around, but could not see anything in the darkness except for the shadowy outline of the trees along the creek.

Gill reached down and touched the bandana he had wrapped around his thigh to help stop the bleeding. He wasn't sure if the bandana was wet from the creek or if his leg was still bleeding, but it didn't really matter. For the first time in three days, he would have a chance to check his injury and clean it.

Looking around, about all he could make out was the outline of his horse. It was standing in the creek only a few feet from him getting a much needed drink. Gill rolled over and took a drink of the clean clear water. He had not had anything to eat or drink for three days. His first thought was he had escaped the men who were after him, but where had he escaped to? He had no idea.

Gill thought about building a fire to heat some water so he could clean his wound, but if his enemy was still following him, a fire at night might lead them right to him. After getting a drink, he pulled himself out of the creek onto the grass. He laid down and closed his eyes, but sleep did not come to him easily. Although the pain in his leg was not as sharp as it had been, it was now a dull ache. Finally, sleep did come.

When morning came, Gill woke to a sun just coming over the ridge to the east, and to the throbbing pain in his leg. He sat up and looked around. Gill quickly discovered that his horse was standing in the thick grass near the edge of the creek, and he appeared to be sleeping. His horse needed to rest as much as he did.

Gill called to his horse. It took several soft calls to get the horse to come to him. Once the horse was standing next to Gill, he reached up and grabbed the stirrup. He pulled himself up and stood on one leg while leaning against the horse. Gill loosened the cinch around the horse's belly. As soon as he got it lose, he took hold of the horse's mane then pulled the saddle off the horse and let it fall to the ground. He took the rope off the saddle and slipped the end over the horse's head, then removed the bridle. Gill limped his way over to the only tree close by and tied the rope to the tree. The rope was long enough to give the horse enough slack so it was able to graze.

He limped back to his saddle bags and removed a pair of pants and a shirt. Gill also took out a clean bandana from the saddle bags. He took off his clothes then limped into the creek where he took a bath and carefully cleaned the wound in his leg. The cool water of the stream felt good as it flowed over and around his wound.

As soon as he was done bathing, he hobbled back to the grass where he had spent the night. He wrapped the wound with the clean bandana, then dressed.

Gill considered himself lucky that the bullet had passed through his leg, missing the bone, and had not cut any major veins or arteries. Even so, it was very painful to walk or even move his leg.

Gill took his rifle and bedroll from the saddle then shuffled his way over to the tree. He sat down and spread out his bedroll then laid down to rest. He laid the rifle across his lap, looked around then closed his eyes. All the moving around had been difficult for him, plus the loss of blood made him feel weak. It also caused his wounded leg to ache. He was hungry, but he was too tired to build a fire and fix something to eat.

He found it was hard for him to fall asleep with the pain and aching in his leg and the emptiness in his stomach. Gill rested for about an hour, but did not sleep. Gradually the pain subsided and he felt like he might be able to move around a bit.

Gill gathered a few small branches that were lying around the base of the tree he had been resting against. He built a small fire. While the fire was burning down to coals, he got some salt pork and a small frypan out of his saddlebags. Gill also got out a few hardtack biscuits. He cooked the salt pork then had biscuits dipped in the grease from the pork and pieces of the salt pork for breakfast. He got some water from the creek in his small coffee pot and brewed some coffee.

One look at his food supply showed him that he had little to eat. It was becoming clear that he would have to find a source of food before long. It would have to be close by because his injury limited his ability to move around very much.

While sitting under the tree, he sipped his coffee as he looked around. The creek was too shallow for fish, but it was a supply of water for other animals. Maybe some small animal might come to drink and he could kill it for something to eat.

After he finished eating what little he had, Gill stood up using the tree for support. He took his time as he scanned the area looking for anything, or anybody who might be around, but he saw nothing. He sat back down on the ground to rest while he thought about what he was going to do. If only a deer or even a rabbit would come to the creek, he might get something to eat. Letting out a sigh, he sat down and leaned back against the tree.

Time passed slowly as he rested. As long as he sat there and didn't move any more than necessary, the pain in his leg was bearable.

The sun had risen high in the sky when he thought he heard something behind him. Gill took hold of his rifle then rolled over and laid down at the base of the tree. His eyes got big when he saw three men on horseback coming toward the creek. They were too far away for him to be able to identify, but his first thought was they were the men who were after him, Billy, Jarred, and their father, Harold Saxton.

They were the same men who had shot him four days ago, and had chased him out onto the prairie. The three riders suddenly disappeared down into a shallow ravine in the plains.

The next thought that ran through Gill's mind was he was seeing things. The only thing he had had to eat in the past almost four days was the meager breakfast he had several hours ago, plus he had lost a lot of blood.

It wasn't until the three riders suddenly came up out of the shallow ravine that he could see them clearly. He realized they were the men who had shot him, the Saxtons, and he was not seeing things.

The Saxtons were moving rather slowly. Jarred, was looking down at the ground every few minutes. It quickly became obvious what Jarred was looking for, and probably finding, the tracks his horse had made. The horse's tracks would lead them right to him.

Gill quickly looked around to see where his horse was. His horse was standing out in the open, but there was no place where he could hide the horse. Putting him in the creek would not hide him. When he looked back toward the three riders, he saw one of them pointing in his direction. They had probably seen his horse.

The Saxtons stopped. They were talking among them-selves about something. They were talking about how they should approach the horse, and wondering if the man they had shot was in any condition to fight them.

Although Gill could see them talking, it wasn't until they started to separate that he figured out what they were going to do. They were going to spread out in the hope of getting close enough to see if he was there, and to see if he was in any condition to fight.

Jarred started to move off to the left while Billy moved off to the right. The old man stayed in the middle. It was clear they were spreading out to make it more difficult for Gill to get a quick shot at each of them.

Gill knew Jarred was the one who was the best tracker, but Billy was better with a gun. The old man, Harold, was the meanest of the bunch. Killing one of his sons would only make him madder, but killing the old man might cause Jarred and Billy to become reckless and do something that would make them easier targets.

Gill made up his mind. He leveled his rifle and aimed it at the old man. Gill knew his 44-40 caliber Henry Repeater would do the job. As soon as he was sure he had a good clean shot at Harold, he squeezed the trigger. The gun fired and a bullet hit the old man square in the chest before any of them heard the shot. The old man fell backwards and rolled off his horse, falling to the ground with a thud.

The shot was such a surprise to Jarred and Billy that they just sat there for a second. Billy reacted first, and just in time. Gill's second shot missed Billy by only a couple of inches. He dove to the ground with his rifle in his hand. His horse ran off out of harm's way. He put the rifle up to his shoulder and pointed it toward the tree where Gill was hiding.

Jarred jumped down from his horse, but failed to grab his rifle from his saddle scabbard before his horse ran off. He quickly laid down in the grass with his pistol in his hand. He looked over at his father and thought about going to his aid, but it was clear there was nothing he could do for him, he was dead.

"Billy, you okay?"

"Yeah. Did you see where that shot came from?"

"No, but I think it came from that tree," Jarred said. "Daddy's dead. What do we do now?"

There was nothing but quiet. There was no breeze, nothing moving and not a sound of any kind in the quiet. It was as if death, itself, had settled over the prairie. Even time seemed to stand still.

Suddenly, the silence was broken by the sound of a pistol shot. Jarred had become so nervous in the quiet that he had to make some kind of noise, if for no other reason than to break the deadly silence. He had fired a shot from his pistol toward the tree in the hope of getting some kind of a response from Gill. He didn't even hit the tree because he was too far away for a pistol to be affective.

"What are you shootin' at," Billy called out. "You can't hit him from here with a pistol."

"I was hopin' to get him to show himself so you could get a shot at him with your rifle."

Gill had seen where the shot had come from. He knew if Jarred hit anything it would be accidental using a pistol, but a rifle would be different. Gill leveled his rifle to where the shot had come from. The only thing he could see was the slight movement of the buffalo grass. He took careful aim at the spot he was sure Jarred would be, then slowly squeezed the trigger. The Henry rifle recoiled into his shoulder as the gun fired.

The bullet slammed into the ground only a foot or so in front of Jarred, throwing dirt, small stones and pieces of grass in his face. He screamed in pain, dropped his pistol and covered his face with his hands. He could not see because of the dirt in his eyes.

"I'm hit," Jarred screamed. "I'm hit."

Jarred stood up and tried to run, but couldn't see where he was going.

"Get down," Billy yelled. "Get down."

Jarred continued to run until he tripped and fell to the ground. He laid on the ground with his hands over his face.

"I can't see," Jarred called out to Billy. "Help me."

Billy wasn't sure what he should do. His brother needed his help, but if he got up and ran to him, he might get shot. It had become only too clear that Gill knew how to use a rifle and use it well.

Gill watched to see if Billy was going to go to his brother's aid. He was ready in case Billy tried to run to his brother. Gill could see Jarred crawling around on his hands and knees in an effort to find his brother. He could see no reason to kill Jarred since he was not a threat to him as long as he couldn't see.

"Billy, lay your rifle down, stand up and drop your pistol down next to your rifle and I will let you go to help your brother. We can end this now, or you can watch your brother die before I get you."

Billy had seen how good Gill was with a rifle. There was little doubt that he could easily kill Jarred. He looked at his father lying dead in the buffalo grass and his brother, a clear target as he sat in the grass trying to figure out which way he should go to find safety.

"What's it going to be?"

"I'm thinking," Billy yelled.

"Maybe this will help. You see that wild flower about three or four feet from your brother?"

"Yeah, I see it."

"Watch it."

Gill leveled his rifle at Jarred then slowly moved his rifle until he was aiming at the wild flower. He slowly squeezed the trigger. The gun fired and the flower quickly disappeared.

Jarred screamed at the sound of another shot being fired so close to him. He was sure it was fired at him.

"The next one to die will be Jarred."

"Okay. Okay. You win."

Gill watched as Billy slowly stood up, afraid that Gill would shoot him anyway. When there was no shot, he carefully laid his rifle down then unbuckled his holster and let it fall to the ground next to his rifle. He slowly moved toward his brother, still not sure Gill would keep his word.

"Help him up and bring him here. You can wash his eyes out in the creek. Don't do anything stupid," Gill called out.

Gill watched as Billy helped his brother to his feet. Gill watched Billy's every move.

As soon as Billy had wrapped his arm around his brother, he began to move closer to where Gill was waiting. Billy had seen that Jarred still had a small pistol stuck in his belt. While they moved closer to the creek, Billy slipped his hand over the small pistol and moved it behind Jarred's back. Billy hoped Gill had not seen him take the pistol from Jarred's belt.

Gill watched every move they made. He noticed that Billy had moved a hand behind Jarred's back. He was sure he was planning something.

As soon as they got close enough where a pistol would be useful, Gill drew his pistol and set his rifle against the tree, never taking his eyes off Billy. Gill knew if Billy was going to try something, it would be now.

Billy suddenly shoved Jarred off to the side, causing him to fall to the ground. At the same time, Billy started to come up with the small pistol, but he was too slow. Gill had been ready. He fired one shot hitting Billy in the gut. The .45 caliber slug from Gill's pistol knocked Billy to the ground.

Billy grabbed his stomach and looked at Gill. There was a surprised look on his face. The expression on his face changed when he realized he was going to die, but it didn't last long. Billy died within a few minutes.

"Billy, did you get him?" Jarred asked, the sound of excitement in his voice.

"No, he didn't," Gill said.

Gill helped Jarred to his feet then walked him to the creek. He sat Jarred down in the water.

"Wash out your eyes as best you can. I doubt you will be able to see, but you might feel better. I'm going to get your horse."

"Don't leave me," Jarred said with a hint of panic in his voice.

"I will not be far. Just stay where you are and you will be fine."

With the injury to his leg, it took Gill several minutes to saddle his horse. He watched as Jarred tried to wash the dirt out of his eyes. Since Gill figured Jarred was not going anywhere, he rode out and gathered the horses and brought them back to where he had camped. Jarred was still sitting in the creek. He was crying.

"Can you see anything?" Gill asked.

"No," he said softly.

"It's probably just as well," Gill said as he helped Jarred get out of the creek.

Gill sat Jarred down next to the tree, then took one of the horses and rode out to get Harold Saxton. Once he had him over the back of the horse, he slowly limped back to his camp. He then loaded Billy over the back of his horse. When Gill was done, he sat down and went through the saddle bags of the Saxtons and found enough food to last several days. He fixed a good meal.

After they ate, he helped Jarred onto his horse then tied one horse to the other. He mounted his horse, picked up the reins of the first horse and started back the way he had come.

After three days of travel, Gill arrived in Dupree where he turned the Saxtons over to the sheriff. He then went to the boarding house where he rested and recuperated from his injury before returning to Pierre. He also collected the reward for the Saxtons.

THE PREACHER AND
MRS. ALLISON

A large freight wagon wound its way down a long narrow, crooked road. The road led from the surrounding hills down into the small town of Silver City in the valley below. When the freight wagon crossed a creek, it arrived in the little town and came to a stop in front of the general store.

Other than the driver, there was one passenger on the freight wagon and his destination was Silver City. He was a tall, lean man in his mid-twenties. The man was dressed in a black suit and wore a black hat with a round flat crown, a flat brim and a plain black hatband. He also wore a black shirt with a white collar.

As soon as the freight wagon stopped, he jumped down off the wagon and stood beside it as he took a minute to look around. From the way the man looked around, he appeared to be looking for something special, rather than just looking the town over.

The wagon driver, impatient to be on his way, called out to the man. When the man turned to look at the driver, the driver tossed his carpet bag down. The man caught the bag and thanked the driver. The driver nodded then yelled at the team of horses and headed out of town leaving the man standing in front of the general store.

As the wagon pulled away, the man stepped up on the boardwalk in front of the store. He stood on the porch and looked up and down the street. There were not many businesses in the small town. Other than the general store, there was an assayer's office, which was to be expected since it was a mining town, a bank, a saloon and what appeared to be a place where a man could get a bath and his back washed by a young woman, for a price.

There were several tents near the edge of the creek. The new arrival noticed a little man in front of one of the tents. The little man was washing clothes in a big tub, then hanging them to dry on a line stretched between two trees. The little man had a long braid of hair down his back and a funny looking cap with no brim. His clothes appeared strange as well. There were no buttons on the jacket, but on it there was fancy stitching of dragons, tigers and a few delicate flowers. The new arrival was sure the little man was a Chinaman doing laundry for those who didn't want to wash their own clothes. He admired the little man for doing such hard work. He also thought that the little man was probably making a better living than most of the miners.

After looking around for several minutes, the tall man turned and went inside the general store. Inside the store was a short man with curly brown hair standing behind a counter. He had an apron on over dark pants and a white shirt. He wore glasses that hung low on his nose and had a pencil stuck behind his right ear. He was obviously the owner of the general store.

"Good afternoon," the owner of the store said with a smile. "Is there somethin' I can help you find?"

"Good afternoon, sir. My name is Anthony Shepard. I'm the new preacher."

"Oh, it's nice to meet you. I'm Will Parker. I own this store. I heard we were getting a new preacher, but they never told us when you would get here."

"I was wondering if you could tell me where I might find the church. I didn't see one when I came into town."

"Well, you see, we don't exactly have one; that is, not yet, anyway," Mr. Parker said sheepishly.

"It was my understanding I would be living in the back of the church. If you don't have a church, then where am I to live, until one is built?"

"Well, you see, we haven't had a preacher for the last six or seven months. The last preacher we had didn't stay too long. In fact, he stayed just long enough to run off with the funds we were raising for the new church."

"I see," Reverend Shepard said thoughtfully. "That still doesn't answer my question."

"No. I guess it doesn't, Reverend," Mr. Parker said, rubbing his chin.

"I don't suppose you have a boarding house in town. I didn't see one when I arrived."

"Well, we don't exactly have one of them, neither. Now, Mrs. Allison, she takes in boarders from time to time. I'm sure she would put you up at her place. She's a widow lady that lives down the street in that two story house you might have seen when you first came into town."

"Would she be home now?"

"I'm pretty sure she would. Just go down the street to the only two story house in town, the one with the porch across the front, and knock on the door. If she ain't there, she'll be at doc's office. She sometimes helps him with the sick or injured, you know," Mr. Parker said.

Reverend Shepard obviously didn't know, but he thanked Mr. Parker, picked up his carpet bag and left the store. While walking down the street toward Mrs. Allison's home, he was thinking it was nice of her to help the doctor. She must be a very nice lady to do that, he thought.

As he walked down the street toward the only two story house in town, he noticed a small building about ten feet off the street. It had been built between two good sized cottonwood trees and was not much bigger than a shed. There was a crudely painted sign above the small door that read "Jail". One of the trees also had a sign on it which read "Hangin' Tree". The one thing the reverend had not seen was any sign that would indicate there was a sheriff's office in town.

The rest of the town was made up of a few log cabins and wooden houses. He was sure most of them were owned by the business owners and those providing services to the miners. The creek was lined with tents that appeared to be where most of the miners lived.

Reverend Shepard was sure the miners were mining not only in the creeks but also in the nearby hills for silver and gold. The preacher had no idea if the miners were actually finding anything of value; but if they were, what they made from mining was probably ending up in the pockets of the owner of the saloon, or the women working in the saloon.

When the preacher arrived at Mrs. Allison's home, he stood in the street and looked up at the biggest building in the town. It was a very nice and well-kept home. He was a little concerned about staying in a house with just a widow lady living there. It might not go over very well with the congregation of his new church, especially the women of the congregation. But on the other hand, if she rented rooms out, there might be others living there.

With such a large house, Reverend Shepard was reasonably certain she probably rented rooms to several people. The house had a large porch across the front just like Mr. Parker had said. There were several chairs neatly arranged in small conversational groupings indicating there might be several people living in the house. That thought made him feel a little more at ease about staying there.

He stepped up on the porch, set his carpet bag on a chair next to the door, then reached up and knocked on the door. While he waited for someone to come to the door, he looked around to see if anyone was watching him. He turned and looked at the door when he heard the door latch, then watched as the door opened.

Standing just inside the house was a tall slender woman with long blond hair, a smooth fair complexion and a broad smile. She was wearing a beautiful light blue satin robe with a tie around her narrow waist. The robe was open down the front almost to her waist. Under the robe, he could see she had on what appeared to be a very thin lacey nightgown that did very little to cover her and showed a good amount of cleavage. It surprised the preacher to see such a beautiful young woman standing in front of him, especially wearing such revealing garments.

"May I help you," she asked as she quickly looked him over, finding him to be rather handsome.

"Ah - - ah, yes, ma'am," he finally said after catching his breath. "Are you Mrs. Allison?"

"Yes, I am. How can I help you?"

"I'm the new preacher, and ah - -, I need a place to stay until the new church is built. I was told you rent rooms."

"Won't you come in?"

"Ah - -, yes, ma'am," he said, not sure it was a good idea for him to go into her house, especially if he was seen by any of the women of his new congregation.

"Please, come with me to the parlor," she said as she stepped back so he could enter the house.

The preacher took a quick look around, then quickly stepped inside. Once he was inside the house, Mrs. Allison led him to a room next to the front door. The preacher followed her into the room and stopped suddenly. He was amazed by what he saw. The room had red flocked wallpaper with gold trim. The windows were covered with very nice red and gold drapes with gold braided tie-backs revealing white sheers. There was a large marble fireplace with a large painting in a fancy gold frame above it.

It was the painting that caught the reverend's attention. The painting over the fireplace was a life size painting of a woman scantly clad in a very sheer nightgown and reclining on a settee. The painting left nothing to the imagination. He had never seen anything like it. The reverend just stood there staring at it with his mouth open.

Mrs. Allison stood next to him and watched him as he looked at the painting. The expression on the reverend's face caused her to smile. She was sure he had never seen a painting quite like it.

"Do you like the painting?" she asked with a slight chuckle in her voice.

"Oh, yes," he said with a soft whisper in his voice.

He suddenly realized what he had said and turned to look at her. He was feeling a little embarrassed and his face turned red, but it only got worse when he realized the painting was of Mrs. Allison.

"I hope the painting doesn't make you uncomfortable."

"Ah - - No - - ma'am - - I was - - just admiring it," he said, then realized he should have said it differently.

"I'm sorry," he said then decided it might be best if he just shut up.

It was clear to her that the painting made him very nervous and embarrassed him. She decided it might be best if they talked in another room that didn't have such a distraction.

"Why don't we go into the kitchen? I think you will be more comfortable there," she suggested.

"Yes. Thank you. I think that is a good idea," he said then followed her into the kitchen.

"I think this will be more comfortable for you," Mrs. Allison said as they walked into the kitchen.

Reverend Shepard waited for Mrs. Allison to sit down before he sat down on the other side of the large table. He looked at her for a moment or so before he felt he could speak without making a fool of himself.

"I am in need of a place to live until the church can be built," he said, then took a moment to catch his breath and think about what he should say.

"I do rent rooms occasionally," she said with a soft smile.

"I was hoping to find a room to rent here, but I'm not sure it's a good idea if I live here," he said hoping his comment would not offend her.

"I think I can understand your concerns," she said with a smile. "I think I can solve your problem as well. There is a room at the back of the house. It has a door that leads directly outside. You would be able to come and go freely without having to go through the main part of the house. Would that interest you?"

"Sort of a private entrance?"

"Yes. A private entrance. The only time you would need to come into the rest of the house would be for your meals. You could come in the door that leads directly into the kitchen from the outside, or you could come into the kitchen from the inside door if the weather is not good, if you prefer."

"That might work," the reverend said as he thought about her solution to his problem.

"I don't see you have much choice, Reverend. There is no place else for you to stay in this town unless you sleep under the trees, or you buy a tent to sleep in like the miners. I might add it will take almost a month to get a tent. You would have to order it from Mr. Parker. I'm sure he doesn't have one in the store."

"Do you have any other guests in your home at this time?"

"Not tonight, but I sometimes take in boarders."

He sat across the table from her and thought about his situation. He really didn't have much choice. He also didn't have the funds to pay for a room.

"I can't pay you anything for awhile. I need to get my congregation organized and find a place to hold services."

"I think we can work that out, too. Are you handy, I mean can you fix things?"

"Yes. I have done a little carpentry work and gardening. I can fix most things, if that's what you mean."

"That is what I mean. I could use a little help taking care of this big house."

"Maybe I could work off my room and board, if that would be acceptable," Reverend Shepard suggested.

"That would be helping me a lot. How about if I make up a list of some of the things I need done. You can work on them when you have time. I don't want to keep you from your duties as a preacher," she said with a smile.

"That would be great," he said feeling a little better. "By the way, do you know who is on the committee in charge of building the church? I would like to find out where we will meet until the church is built."

"Mr. Parker is head of the church committee. He owns the general store."

"Yes, I have met him. If we are done for now, I would like to see the room and get settled in."

"Certainly," Mrs. Allison said as she stood up.

Reverend Shepard stood and followed her to a room just off the kitchen. They went inside. While Reverend Shepard looked around the room, Mrs. Allison sat down on the edge of the bed. The first thing Reverend Shepard saw was that there was a door on the outside wall with a window next to it. He could see it led out onto a large porch. There was a desk and chair under the window next to the door.

The next thing he saw was the rather large four poster bed with a night stand next to it. He hardly noticed anything other than the bed since Mrs. Allison was casually reclining on it. He turned a little red with embarrassment seeing her reclining on the bed and smiling at him, especially with what she was wearing. He quickly turned away. It took a moment for him to regain his composure.

"Ah - - This will be fine," he said then he turned and looked at Mrs. Allison.

Mrs. Allison smiled when he looked at her. It was clear to her that he was embarrassed to be in a bedroom with her. She was sure it was the way she was dressed and the fact that she was reclining on the bed that embarrassed him. She thought it might be best if she left him to get settled in. She stood up and gracefully walked over to the door that led into the kitchen. She turned and looked at him.

"I'll leave you for now so you can get settled in," she said with a smile.

"Thank you," he said as he watched her leave the room, shutting the door behind her.

Reverend Shephard just stood there looking at the door after it closed. He took a deep breath as he tried to get the vision of her out of his head. He turned around, then took a few minutes to look around the room before he went out the door at the back of the house. He walked all the way around the house to the front porch where he had left his carpet bag. After retrieving his carpet bag, he carried it around to the back of the house and into his room. He set the carpet bag on the bed then sat down at the desk and looked out the window.

Reverend Shephard wasn't really looking at the small stable behind the house. He was thinking about Mrs. Allison. He had never seen a woman who was so beautiful and so desirable. She didn't appear to be more than about three or four years older than him.

His thoughts turned to the fact she was a widow. He wondered what had happened to her husband, but didn't think it was any of his business.

He decided it might be a good idea if he had a talk with Mr. Parker at the general store. Reverend Shepard left his room and walked down the street to the general store. When he walked in, he saw Mr. Parker writing something in a book while standing behind the counter. The reverend looked around to see if there was anyone else in the store. He didn't see anyone.

"Is there something I can do for you, Reverend?" Mr. Parker asked when he looked up and saw the reverend looking around the store.

"Yes, Mr. Parker, there is. I understand you are one of the elders of the church. Is that correct?"

"Yes. Why don't you call me, Will? Everyone in town calls me Will."

"Okay, Will. I would like to know where we hold church services since we do not have a church."

"Well, we haven't actually held any services since the last preacher left, you understand."

"Yes. I understand. Where did you hold them while he was here?"

"Well, when the weather was cooperating, we held them outside on the front yard of Mrs. Allison's place. Her front yard's very nice."

"I noticed. It's a very nice yard. When the weather didn't cooperate?"

"Well, we held them in the parlor at Mrs. Allison's place."

"You held them where?" the reverend said wondering if he had heard Mr. Parker correctly.

"In the parlor at Mrs. Allison's home."

"In the parlor?" Reverend Shepard asked with a shocked tone in his voice. "That doesn't seem like an appropriate place to hold church services with that painting hanging above the fireplace."

"Oh, we covered the painting before the children came in."

"I'm glad to hear that," Reverend Shepard said feeling somewhat relieved.

"We didn't want the children to be distracted by it, you know."

"I'm sure. When did you hold church, by that I mean what time on Sunday?"

"Well, I guess that's up to you, of course, but we usually held services at about eleven in the morning, Sunday morning, of course."

"Of course. Isn't that kind of late?"

"Not many of the folks get up real early around here on Sunday morning," Will said.

"And why is that?" Reverend Shepard asked, having a good idea of what the answer would be.

"Well, you see, it's like this. Folks around here work hard all week. Ah - they tend to sleep in on Sunday morning."

"In other words, they, shall we say, celebrate the end of the work week on Saturday night and are unable to get up any earlier."

"I think that's about the best way I've heard it put," Will said with a grin.

"Will you be so kind as to tell our congregation there will be Sunday services at Mrs. Allison's home at eleven o'clock? The services will be outside if the weather permits."

"Yes, sir. I certainly will tell them."

Reverend Shepard left the general store and returned to his room. He sat down at the desk in his room and began working on his sermon for Sunday. It was a long time before he actually put pen to paper. His mind was all over the place. He was sure he had been sent to this place because he had upset someone higher up in the church's hierarchy. It crossed his mind that he had been sent to this place to spend some time in hell in order to make him a better preacher.

It was also hard for him to get Mrs. Allison off his mind. She was the most beautiful woman he had ever seen, and she was very nice, too.

Just as he was about to write his greeting to his new congregation, he heard a loud scream coming from the kitchen. He immediately dropped his pen, pushed back from the desk and ran out of his room into the kitchen. He was shocked at what he saw. There was a big man holding Mrs. Allison by the arm while he slapped her across the face.

"Stop that!" Reverend Shepard yelled at the man.

To the reverend's surprise, the big man stopped and looked at him. When the man saw who was yelling at him, he started to grin.

"Mind your own business, little preacher man."

"Hitting anyone who can't fight back is my business," the reverend said.

The big man just looked at the reverend and began to laugh. After a short laugh, the big man looked at the reverend, his face turning serious.

"Get lost," the man said sharply.

He turned away from the reverend then raised his hand to strike Mrs. Allison again. He had just started to swing his hand when the reverend lunged forward and grabbed the man's hand. The big man was so surprised that he let go of Mrs. Allison and stepped back. He looked at the reverend with hate in his eyes.

The man reached out and grabbed the reverend by the front of his shirt then hit him in the face, knocking him to the floor. He then stood there looking at the reverend, grinning from ear to ear.

"You want some more?" the big man asked.

"No," the reverend said. "But I will not let you beat on a woman who obviously can't defend herself and doesn't want you here."

"What is it you preachers are supposed to do? Oh, I remember, it's turn the other cheek."

"That would be correct," the reverend said as he stood up.

The big man grinned as he watched the reverend. As soon as the reverend was on his feet, the big man started to move closer. He drew back his fist and started to swing at the reverend, but the reverend ducked the swing and planted a fist into the big man's belly causing the big man to double over. The reverend finished with a hard uppercut to the big man's chin causing him to fall backward onto the floor. He was out cold.

The reverend looked at the big man for a moment, then looked at Mrs. Allison. He could see the surprised look on her face.

"I'm sorry you had to see that. I guess I just can't stand to see a man beat a woman. By the way, who is he?"

"He's Big Mike, the town bully. He likes to beat up on people."

Mrs. Allison quickly moved next to the reverend, reached up and lightly touched the bruise on his face.

"Let me help you," she said as she took him by the arm and guided him to a chair.

After he was seated at the table, she went to the sink and pumped some water into it. She wet a cloth then she went to him and gently placed the cool cloth over the bruise.

The reverend flinched a bit when she first put the cloth on his bruise, but the coolness of the cloth did feel good. He couldn't help watching her. He noticed she had a red mark on her face from where Big Mike had slapped her. He had to grin.

"We are a pair," he said as he reached out and lightly touch the mark on her face.

"Yes. We are," she said with a smile as she looked into his eyes.

Mrs. Allison slowly leaned toward him. Holding the damp cloth on his bruise, she kissed him lightly on the cheek then leaned back.

Reverend Shepard looked at her for a moment then smiled at her. He slowly leaned toward her and kissed her on the lips.

Just then they heard a groan from Big Mike. They quickly stood up, stepped back away from each other and got ready to defend themselves, but Big Mike didn't get up. He was still out cold.

"What do we do about him?" Mrs. Allison asked when the big man didn't move.

"I saw a jail on my way over here. Is there a sheriff or marshal in this town?"

"No. The miners ran him out of town about a week ago."

"I think I will take him over to the jail and lock him up until he sobers up."

"I think that is a good idea," she said with a smile.

The reverend reached down, grabbed Big Mike by the scruff of his neck and dragged him out the back of the house. There was a wheelbarrow leaning against the corner of the house. The reverend got the wheelbarrow and put Big Mike in it, then started down the street toward the jail.

He hadn't gone very far when several people saw him pushing the wheelbarrow with Big Mike in it toward the jail. They immediately followed him to see what their new preacher was going to do with Big Mike.

When the reverend arrived at the jail, he discovered that he had been followed. He didn't say anything to those who stood behind him. He simply opened the door to the jail, wheeled Big Mike into the jail, unceremoniously dumped him out of the wheelbarrow onto the dirt floor then closed the door. There wasn't a lock on the door, but there was a place where a board could be put across the door to keep it closed, and the board was leaning against the wall next to the door. He barred the door, then turned around and looked at four or five men who had seen him lock up Big Mike. They were looking at him as if they expected him to say something. He decided to oblige them.

"Church services will be at Mrs. Allison's home at eleven o'clock sharp on Sunday morning. I expect to see all of you there," he said firmly, then turned and wheeled the empty wheelbarrow back to Mrs. Allison's home where he leaned it against the house where he had found it.

He went inside where Mrs. Allison greeted him with a cup of coffee. He had just sat down at the kitchen table next to Mrs. Allison to enjoy a quiet cup of coffee with her when there was a knock on the backdoor. Mrs. Allison looked at Anthony wondering who could be at her door at this hour. She got up and answered the door. Much to her surprise, there were four men standing on her back porch.

"We want to talk to the reverend," one of the men said standing at the door with his hat in his hand.

"Come in, gentlemen," she said then turned to the reverend. "There are some gentlemen here to see you."

The men came into the kitchen. The one leading them was Will Parker.

"What is it you gentlemen want?"

"We'll get right to the point, Reverend," Will Parker said. "We saw what you did to Big Mike. We want you to be the town marshal."

"But I'm a preacher, not a lawman," he reminded them.

"You sure are. You did more to inspire this town to go to church than anyone I ever seen. You could be a preacher on Sunday and a lawman during the week. Besides, the job of lawman pays. I can't say you'll make anything as a preacher in this town."

Reverend Shepard looked at each of the men standing in front of him. He didn't know what to think. He turned and looked at Mrs. Allison. She was smiling at him.

"What do you think?" he asked her.

"I think it's a good idea. I would like it if you stay here with me."

That very afternoon Reverend Shepard became Marshal Shepard during the week, but on Sunday morning he was the town's preacher who preached fire and brimstone to the miners and the town folks.

Silver City quickly became a quiet little town with Marshal Shepard watching over it during the week, and Reverend Shepard watching over the souls of the people on Sunday. The Sunday service was always full.

After a few weeks, Anthony Shepard married Mrs. Allison. They moved the painting of her from the parlor to their bedroom where only they could enjoy it. And as the story goes, they lived happily ever after.

A CHASE INTO THE BACKCOUNTRY

The Cheyenne to Deadwood Stagecoach left Newcastle, in the Wyoming Territory, for Custer City in the Dakota Territory. The stagecoach was making good time as it moved swiftly along the road. Once it was in the Dakota Territory, it would not be long before it would have to slow down in the hills and valleys leading to its destination.

Up ahead was a portion of the road that was rather narrow and very crooked. It was well known as the most dangerous part of the trip, not only because of the crooked narrow road, but because the stagecoach had been robbed several times in the area.

There were six people on the stagecoach that afternoon-- the driver, a guard riding shotgun on top of the stagecoach, and four passengers inside the stagecoach. Inside there was a gambler on his way to Deadwood, a young woman on her way to Hill City to meet a man she was going to marry, a salesman hoping to sell his wares in Custer City and a bounty hunter. The bounty hunter was looking for a man who had murdered several people over the past couple of years during robberies of two banks and three stagecoaches on different stagecoach lines.

Since the stagecoach was not the most comfortable ride, there had been very little talking among the passengers. It wasn't until they approached the most dangerous part of the road that anyone spoke, and the first to speak was the young woman going to Hill City.

"Excuse me, sir," she said to the man sitting next to her.

The bounty hunter was the passenger sitting next to the young woman. He looked at her and smiled.

"What can I do for you, ma'am?"

"Is it true that the stagecoach is often held up by highwaymen along this route?"

"Yes, it is, but I wouldn't worry too much about it. We have a man riding shotgun, and there are two well armed men riding inside the stagecoach."

"One of those men in the stagecoach is known to be very handy with a gun," the salesman said, then looked at Sam. "He is Sam Edson, a bounty hunter."

The young woman looked from the salesman to Sam. She looked at Sam as if he was some sort of strange animal. She wasn't sure how she felt about being in the confines of a stagecoach with a man who hunted other men for money. It took her a couple minutes of thought to realize that should they have trouble, having someone with his obvious abilities and skill with a gun might be helpful.

"I'm sorry if what I do offends you," Sam said seeing the look on her face, "but I can assure you I don't take it lightly. I always try to take the outlaws in alive, even if the wanted poster offers a reward for them dead or alive."

"I'm sorry if I judged you. I'm sure you perform a needed service to help keep this country safe for others."

"I think I do since there are very few lawmen out here to cover such a large part of the country. The lawmen here in the west are often limited by the confines of their jurisdiction. I am not."

"Sam!" the driver called out, interrupting them.

"Yeah."

"Keep an eye open. We're comin' to the narrow part of this here trip."

"Okay," Sam said as he looked at the young woman.

The young woman just looked at him then smiled. It had not occurred to her that he was on the stagecoach to help protect it from robbers.

"Not everything I do is hunting bad men," he said with a smile.

Sam looked out the window on his side of the stagecoach for a moment, then turned and looked at the gambler sitting across from him. At first, he didn't think much about the gambler, but he did notice the gambler was looking at him.

He took a moment or two before he looked back out the side window. Thoughts about the gambler were running through Sam's head. He couldn't remember where he had seen the gambler before, but he was sure he had seen him. It could have been almost any place in or around the Black Hills. It might have been on a wanted poster, but he just wasn't sure.

He slowly turned his head. As he did, he looked at the gambler again; but continued to turn his head so he could look out the other side of the stagecoach.

While Sam appeared to be looking out the window on the far side of the stagecoach, he also glanced at the salesman. He did remember seeing him a while back in one of the saloons. If he remembered correctly, he had seen the salesman in Hill City a few weeks ago. Sam had seen him with the same sample box lying at the salesman's feet. It occurred to him that he had never seen the salesman sell anything. From what he had heard and seen, the salesman had spent all his time in Hill City gambling in the Silver Dollar saloon.

It suddenly came to Sam where he had seen the gambler before. The gambler had been sitting across the table from the salesman playing poker. The two of them had been in town just two days before the bank in Custer City was held up. If he remembered correctly, they both left town early on the morning of the robbery.

Sam had to think about it. He didn't really have any-thing to go on to take them into custody so they could be turned over to a lawman. If they were the ones who held up the bank in Custer City, there would be a reward for their capture. As far as he knew, there were no wanted posters out on them so there wasn't much he could do. There was also the possibility they had not done anything against the law. All he had to go on was his gut feeling. If he arrested them based on his gut feeling, it would not hold up in court. About the only thing he could do was to watch them and be ready for anything they might do so he was not caught off guard.

Suddenly there was a yell from the driver of the stagecoach for the horses to stop. The sudden feel of the stagecoach braking caused those facing forward to slide off their seats and toward those with their backs to the front. It caught everyone off balance including Sam. The young woman slid off the seat and fell in the salesman's lap while Sam was caught off balance and had to reach out to protect himself from falling.

In the confusion of the moment, the gambler drew his gun from under his coat and pointed it at Sam. Sam looked toward the gambler only to find a gun in his face.

"I think you should hand over your gun," the gambler said calmly. "I wouldn't do anything foolish. You could get someone hurt."

The gambler reached out his free hand for Sam's gun. There was little else Sam could do. He handed his gun to the gambler.

"Now what?" Sam asked as he straightened up and sat back on the seat.

"Now that the stagecoach has stopped, I want the driver and the guard to toss their guns down on the ground."

Sam looked at the gambler for a moment before calling out, "Will, we got a problem in here. It would be a good idea if you drop your weapons down on the ground."

"What the hell?" Will said.

"We're being robbed and I would hate to see this young woman get hurt. I suggest you do as he ordered," Sam said.

The passengers could feel the stagecoach rock a little followed by the thud of the guns hitting the ground.

"Now everyone get out of the stagecoach," the gambler said. "You first, young lady."

The young woman looked at Sam, then moved to the door and got out of the stagecoach. She was followed by the salesman, then Sam.

Once the passengers were out of the stagecoach, the gambler got out and had the passengers sit down on the ground with their backs to him. He ordered the driver and the guard to get down.

As soon as everyone was on the ground, the gambler ordered the driver and guard to move the log from in front of the stagecoach. As soon as the log was moved, he again had everyone sit down on the ground. When all were seated on the ground, the gambler climbed up onto the driver's seat. He released the hand break, then yelled for the horses to get moving. The stagecoach lunged forward and took off. It rounded a corner and was soon out of sight.

Sam turned just in time to see it disappear from sight. He let out a sigh of disappointment as he stood up.

"It's okay. You can stand up," Sam said.

All the passengers stood up then looked around. It was clear they had no idea what they were to do, or how they were going to get where they were going.

"Excuse me, Mr. Edson, but what do we do now?" the woman asked.

"I guess you have two choices. One, you can start walking, but it will take you at least three days to get to the next town, Custer City. Or you could make yourselves as comfortable as possible and wait for someone to come and get you, which could take two days."

"What are you going to do?" she asked thinking that he had something else in mind.

"Well, ma'am, I'm going to walk down this road about a mile and get my horse."

The young woman just looked at him. She was a little confused by his comment.

"You mean you have a horse about a mile from here?"

"Yes, ma'am," he admitted as if it was something she should have expected.

"You knew this stagecoach was going to be robbed, and it was going to be robbed on this section of road, is that right?" she asked with a hint of anger in her voice.

"Not really. I had a good idea that it might be robbed based on the number of times it has been robbed along here. It has been awhile since it was robbed on this route. It was a guess on my part. I guess you could say I played a hunch."

"If you have just one horse, then it seems clear to me that you are going to leave us here while you go after the stagecoach."

Sam looked at the rest of them as they sat on some rocks and listened to the young woman while she looked at him. He reached down and pulled a small pistol out of his boot, then walked closer to the group.

"Actually, I have two horses. I'm going to take Wilbur Sterns with me. Standup Wilbur," Sam said as he pointed the gun at the salesman.

The salesman stood up. Everyone was wondering what was going on.

"Wilbur just happens to be Josh Sterns' partner and his father. The man who robbed the stagecoach was Josh Sterns. They were in on this together," Sam said.

"You knew who they were all the time," the young woman declared.

"No, ma'am, I didn't. I didn't put it together until I saw the gun. It was one of those shiny and very expensive new Colts. It was the one thing that caused me to remember who it was sitting across from me," he explained.

"I'm sorry, but I have to be going. The longer I stand here talking, the harder it is going to be for me to catch up with Josh Sterns. By the way, if you start walking, you might find the stagecoach along the road, probably within the next two miles. It would be my guess Sterns wouldn't want to drive the stagecoach very far. It doesn't make the fastest way to get away, and it doesn't travel well off the roads."

Sam turned and gave Wilbur a shove to get him moving. Wilbur stumbled a little, but began to walk when Sam gave him another shove.

"If you don't move it along, when we get to my horses, I will tie you across the saddle like a sack of potatoes for the ride into Custer City."

Reluctantly Wilbur started to walk. He tried to move as slow as he could, but every time he tried to slow Sam down, he got a good hard jab in the back with the barrel of Sam's pistol. It took a little over half an hour to get to where Sam's horses had been left by a friend of his.

He put Wilbur on a horse and shackled him to the saddle horn. He swung into the saddle of the other horse, grabbed the reins and started off down the road. They hadn't gone very far when they came to the deserted stagecoach.

Sam was correct. He was sure it wouldn't take the others very long to get to the stagecoach.

Since the lead horses had been tied to a tree, Sam was sure the stagecoach would not be going anywhere before the other passengers could find it. Sam continued on toward Custer City. He was sure Josh Sterns would go there, get some supplies then head into the backcountry of the Black Hills where he would wait for Wilbur to show up. If Josh got into the backcountry of the Black Hills, it would be almost impossible to find him.

Sam rode into Custer City with Wilbur in tow. He went directly to the sheriff's office. He just stepped out of the saddle when the sheriff stepped out of his office.

"Hey, I thought you were on the stagecoach that was due almost two hours ago," the sheriff said.

"I was. The stagecoach was held up by one of the passengers. A guy by the name of Josh Sterns, with the help of his father, held it up. Let's get this guy locked up. He's the father of Josh Sterns, Wilbur Sterns."

The sheriff took Wilbur into the jail and locked him up in a cell.

"That should keep him for a while," the sheriff said.

"Have you seen Sterns?"

"He's that gambler fella, ain't he?"

"Yeah. He had a horse hidden just a short distance from where my horses had been hidden."

"Well, I seen him walkin' from the general store with some supplies just a little while ago. He was walkin' just as calm as you please toward the livery stable. He sure didn't act like he had just robbed the stagecoach."

"Maybe not, but he did. Did you see which way he went when he left town?" Sam asked.

"Not for sure, but he looked like he might be goin' toward Hill City."

"I doubt he will go into Hill City. He's more likely to go into the backcountry. He knows the word will get out fast, and a lot of people know him around there. It wouldn't surprise me if he leaves the territory as soon as he knows what happened to his father. He will probably plan a way to rescue his father before he leaves the area, though."

"You think he will come here and try to get him out of jail?" the sheriff asked.

"He might, but I doubt he will try anything soon. He will know he has time to plan the escape of his father. I'm sure he knows it will take time to get a judge here and have a trial."

"What do you want me to do?"

"Keep Wilbur locked up and don't allow him any visitors. Keep a guard on him at all times."

"Okay," the sheriff said. "What are you goin' to do?"

"I'm going to try to find Josh."

"You goin' into the backcountry alone?"

"I don't have time to get a posse together. A lot of men looking for him might just scare him off, then we might never find him. He seems to know the backcountry pretty well."

"I'm sure you're right. I'll keep an eye on this one for you."

"Thanks, I need to get going," Sam said.

Sam shook the sheriff's hand, then left the Sheriff's Office. He took his horses to the livery stable and left them there.

While his horses were fed, watered and rubbed down by the owner of the livery stable, Sam went to the general store. He picked up enough supplies for what he was sure he would need for the several days it would probably take him to find and capture Josh. Sam returned to the livery stable, and saddled one of his horses. As soon as he stowed his supplies in his saddle bags, he swung into the saddle and was ready to go after Josh.

Sam slowly rode north out of town looking for tracks from Josh's horse. He had made it a point to study the tracks of the horse as he rode toward Hill City. He had noticed that one of the horse's shoes, the right front shoe, had a nick in the toe of the horseshoe. He knew it would not be easy to follow, but it was all he had to go on.

He was about a mile and a half out of Custer City when he noticed an area in the road that looked like someone had pushed the dirt around with his boot. Sam took a minute to look at it. He quickly discovered that the hoof prints in the dirt with the nick in them had been rubbed out. They did not continue down the road past where all the tracks had been brushed out. It was clear that Josh had tried to cover his tracks in order to keep anyone from following him.

Sam got off his horse, then slowly began walking around the area looking at the ground and hoping he might find a new set of tracks. It didn't take him very long to figure out that Josh had turned off the road and headed across a pasture toward the trees. Once in the trees, it would be harder to follow him as the pine needles on the ground would make it hard to read hoof prints.

Sam stood next to his horse as he looked toward the trees on the other side of the pasture. If Josh was watching him from the trees, he might be walking into a trap. He turned his head and slowly looked around from up the road to the other side of the road. In doing so, he was able to see that the line of trees came close to the road just a little further down the road. He decided to ride down the road until he was past the tree line, then turn into the woods and work his way back along the tree line in the hope of finding the tracks again.

He stepped up next to his horse, put his foot in the stirrup and swung into the saddle. Sam gently nudged his horse and continued down the road. When he reached the place where the trees met the road, he turned off the road and in among the trees. Once inside the forest, he sat in the saddle and looked around as he listened for any kind of noise that might indicate trouble. He heard nothing.

Lightly patting his horse on the neck, he nudged his horse along the tree line just inside the forest. The horse walked along moving around the trees while staying inside the forest. The horse moved quietly on the pine needle covered forest floor.

Sam hadn't gone very far when a tree branch literally exploded near his head followed by the sharp report of a rifle. He dove off his horse and scrambled behind the trunk of a dead tree. His horse moved off about fifteen feet then stopped.

For several minutes, there was not a sound. Sam looked at his horse. The horse was standing with its ears up while looking in the direction the shot had come from.

"What do you hear?" Sam whispered.

The horse quickly turned his head, looked at Sam, then quickly turned his head back without making a sound. After a couple of minutes, the horse seemed to relax and Sam stood up.

Sam moved up next to his horse and patted him on the neck. He took hold of the reins and began walking deeper into the forest, closer to where the shot had come from. It didn't take Sam long to find the place where the shooter had been. There were signs of shuffling of feet in the pine needles on the ground, and a cartridge casing lying on the ground next to the tree. There were also signs of someone turning and running away from where the cartridge was lying.

"Well, boy. It looks like this is not going to be easy," Sam said as if he expected his horse to understand.

He took the reins of his horse and started following the tracks. It wasn't long and he found where Josh had left his horse. The tracks of the horse leaving the area would not be hard to follow. In fact, they were a little too easy to follow to Sam's way of thinking. It might be another trap. If Josh could get him to follow the tracks of his horse, he could set Sam up for another ambush.

Sam turned and led his horse off away from the tracks. He knew of a place where there where rocky outcroppings and boulders big enough to hid behind. He had discovered it sometime ago while hunting deer in the area. Sam stepped into the saddle and nudged his horse away from the tracks.

After he had gone several hundred yards away from where Josh had shot at him, he turned and rode toward the rocky area. When he was still a good two hundred yards from the rocky area, he stopped. The sudden sound of something behind him caused Sam to dive off his horse and draw his gun. He swung around in time to see a large buck take off and disappear in the woods.

Sam stood up and took a deep breath. He walked over to his horse. He led the horse to a small outcropping of rock where his horse would not be seen. Sam tied his horse to a tree. He moved away from his horse then rolled out his bedroll under the outcropping. He settled down on the bedroll to wait for darkness to come to the forest. Sam made sure he could see his horse from where he had laid out his bedroll. His horse could hear, smell or see anything that might be moving around in the forest long before Sam.

Time passed slowly as the sun set in the west. Once it was dark, Sam moved away from his bedroll just in case he had been spotted. He moved up on top of the outcropping among some large rocks to wait for the moon to come up over the horizon.

It wasn't long before the moon was up in the sky high enough to spread its soft light down through the trees. Sam rested with his back against a boulder.

Suddenly his horse snorted as if he smelled something. It was only a few seconds before Sam smelled the faint odor of smoke. There was a slight breeze coming out of the northwest.

Sam quickly moved away from the boulder and into the shadowy forest. Moving as quietly as possible, he followed the scent of smoke. It wasn't very long before he saw the glow of a small fire, one like someone had built to help keep warm or use to make some coffee.

Being as careful as possible not to make a sound, Sam worked his way closer to the fire. When he was only a few yards from the fire, he could see what looked like a man sitting in front of the fire with a blanket wrapped around him. He watched the man for several minutes, but the man never moved, not even to stir the fire or reach for the coffee pot at the edge of the fire.

The longer Sam watched the man, the more he believed it was not a man, but a dummy. It had been put there in the hope he would shoot it and give away his position, or walk into the camp with his gun drawn expecting to capture the man when he was really walking into a trap.

Sam carefully looked around. He had no idea where Josh was, but to walk into the camp could very well be the last thing he would ever do. He studied the situation and came up with a plan. He laid his rifle among some rocks aiming it at the dummy. He took a pigging string from his belt that he carried for tying up prisoners. He made a loop in the end and hooked it to the trigger of the rifle then moved off to the side. He drew his pistol from his holster, cocked it then readied himself.

As soon as he was ready, he pulled on the string. The rifle fired and the shot hit the dummy. Within a second there was a shot from across the other side of the fire, but the slug struck a tree several feet from Sam. Sam saw the flash from the gun and quickly fired two rounds in that direction. He heard a cry of pain. He was sure he hit Josh, but didn't know how badly he was injured.

"You ready to give it up?" Sam called out.

He didn't get an answer for what seemed like a very long time, but it was only a minute or so.

"I'm hit," Josh said, his voice sounding strained.

"Toss the gun out by the fire where I can see it."

"I can't. I'm hurt bad."

"I'm not coming in after you in the dark. If you're hurt that bad you might bleed to death before morning. Come out where I can see you."

Sam waited for a response, but didn't hear anything for several minutes. There was nothing but silence. He thought about working his way around to where the shot had come from, but thought better of it. Instead, he decided to wait.

Several minutes had passed when he heard a twig snap off to his left. Sam quickly rolled away and fired two shots at where the sound had come from. In the dim light of the moon, he saw a man fall to the ground. He could hear the man groan in pain.

Keeping his gun on the man, Sam stood up and cautiously moved toward him. When he was only two or three feet from the man, he could see it was Josh. The front of his shirt, just above his belt, was red with blood. Josh looked up at Sam.

"I guess you got me," Josh said, his pain showing in his voice.

"I guess I did. Let me see how bad you're hurt."

"No need for that. I'm gut shot," he said as he tried to take a breath.

"I'm sorry about that, but you have to admit you asked for it."

"Yeah."

"Tell me something. Why did you kill the bank teller and the stagecoach driver in those two robberies?"

"They didn't give me a choice," Josh said then coughed.

The pain he was feeling was getting worse. Sam knew it wouldn't be much longer before Josh would die.

"They tried to shoot me," he said, then coughed again.

Sam just sat there and watched Josh. There was no doubt in Sam's mind that Josh was on his way out.

Suddenly, Josh took a shallow breath, closed his eyes and let out his last breath. He was gone.

Sam carried Josh to his bedroll and wrapped him in it. After retrieving his horse and his bedroll, he sat down across the fire from Josh. It was over. Sam laid out his bedroll and went to sleep.

When morning came, Sam took Josh's body and put it over the back of Josh's horse then headed back to Custer City. It was mid-morning when he arrived back in Custer City and claimed his reward. Once he had his money, he got back on his horse and rode to Hill City to spend some time with a female friend.

Sam stayed in Hill City for a few days before he found another wanted poster of someone the law had not been able to catch. He left Hill City in search of another outlaw.

LOVE FINDS A HOME

Love is one of the best feelings a person can have, and it has been that way throughout history. It was no different for David Morgan and the love of his life, Mary Erickson. For Mary and David, there were obstacles they thought could only be overcome by running away together.

David Morgan was a young man of seventeen when he quietly snuck out of his parents' house. He ran around to the back of his father's blacksmith shop and livery stable where his father kept a small covered wagon which could be drawn easily by two horses. Over the past two months, David had hidden a few supplies in the loft of the livery stable.

He quickly loaded what supplies he had into the wagon. His supplies consisted of some food, a few quilts, and a few clothes. He put his rifle and a pistol in the wagon with an extra box of shells for each.

As soon as he had the supplies in the wagon, he harnessed a team of horses then hitched them to the wagon. Taking the reins of the lead horse, he quietly led the horses away from the livery stable and down the road away from his father's blacksmith shop. When he was sure he was far enough away from the livery stable so his father or mother would not be awakened by the sounds of the wagon and the horses, he got up on the seat and drove away.

He moved as quietly as he could across town to the other side of the railroad tracks because he didn't want anyone in town to hear him or see him. When he was a couple of blocks from Mr. Erickson's home, he stopped and tied the horses to a tree. David slipped down along the alley behind the houses until he was at the back of the Erickson house. He moved along the fence that ran between the houses toward the back of the Erickson house.

David knelt down behind a large bush at the back corner of the house to wait for Mary. It seemed to take forever for her to come out. He began to worry that she was not going to be able to get away, or that her father had discovered their plan to run away and would not let her out of the house.

David let out a sigh of relief when he saw Mary come out the backdoor. Mary was a pretty girl of sixteen. She was slender with dark brown hair and brown eyes. David watched her as she quietly shut the door behind her, then tiptoed off the back porch.

As soon as she was off the porch, she ran to the bush where she was to meet David. When she got to him, she threw her arms around David's neck and kissed him. It was a quick kiss as they needed to get away as fast as they could. To be discovered by Mr. Erickson would mean they might never see each other again.

They ran along behind the houses to where David had tied the horses. He helped her onto the wagon, then untied the team of horses. He got up on the wagon seat.

When he started the horses down the street away from the Erickson house, Mary looped her arm in David's as she moved closer to him. He moved the horses slowly in an effort to make as little noise as possible so they would not be heard.

Once they were out of town, they kept on moving. They moved along in the dim light of an almost full moon. They traveled all night, heading west with the hope that Mary's father would not be able to find them. When the sun came up, the wagon with the two young people was still moving west.

David and Mary kept moving all day and into the next night, stopping only occasionally to rest and water the horses and to let them eat. After the sunset on the first full day of travel, they stopped for the night to give the horses a chance to rest. They didn't build a fire for fear that it might be seen. Instead, they ate what they had that didn't need to be cooked. They had intentionally decided to travel light so they could move faster and get as far away as possible before it was discovered they had run away.

After traveling for only a week from sunup to sunset, they discovered they were ill prepared for what lay ahead of them, but they continued on in spite of their lack of preparation for such a long trip. They had not packed enough of the food staples they would need, like sugar, flour, and especially water.

Once out on the open prairie they were finding it harder and harder to find food. They took time to hunt, but David was not skilled at hunting or preparing what he did kill. They did manage to kill a few rabbits and an occasional grouse, but that was about it. It seemed that any animal of any size was too far away for David to get a good shot at. He made an effort to hunt close to their wagon so they didn't have to stop for very long while David hunted.

Water was also scarce. Out on the prairie, the creeks and rivers were few and far between. It had been hard to keep going, but they were set on getting to some place where they could live the way they wanted to live.

They had been traveling for several weeks across the open prairie when David saw what looked like a small town. David wasn't sure he was really seeing the town; but if it was a town, they might find food there.

"Mary, look," he said as he pointed toward what he thought was a small town. "It looks like a town."

"I see it," she said excitedly. "We might be able to get some food there."

"We don't have very much money, but I'm sure we could get something to eat there."

David turned the team of horses and headed toward the small town. The town was further away than he had thought. He wanted to move faster, but his horses were very tired. Maybe they could rest the animals there.

The horses plodded along toward the small town. When they got closer they realized that there were only a few buildings. There was a general store, a saloon, a bank and a blacksmith shop with a livery stable.

David drove the team of horses to the livery stable and stopped. A woman came out of the stable and looked at them.

"Good afternoon," the woman said.

"Good afternoon. I was wondering if we could leave our team of horses here while we get something to eat?" David asked.

"You can, but I can't help you with them. You will have to take care of them yourself. My husband is laid up with a broken leg."

"I'm sorry to hear that. Is your husband a blacksmith?"

"Yes, but he is unable to help you if you need the help of a blacksmith. Besides, he has a lot of work to catch up on as soon as he's able to get around."

"How did he break his leg?" David asked.

"He broke it when he fell from a ladder. He has been laid up for over a week now."

David looked at Mary. He had an idea. Mary smiled.

"We have very little money to buy the things we need, like food for us and feed for the horses. If I was to help in the blacksmith shop and around the stable, would you be willing to help us with what we need?"

"What we really need is a blacksmith," the woman said.

"I am a blacksmith," David said with a smile.

The woman looked at him, not sure she believed him. She thought for a minute or so about what he had said. If he really was a blacksmith, maybe he could be helpful, she thought.

"Why don't you put your horses in the corral, then come to the house. I'm sure my husband would like to talk to you."

"Thank you. By the way, I'm David and this is Mary," he said as he got down from the wagon.

"I'm Martha, and my husband is Stephen."

"Nice to meet you," David said.

"The Mrs. can come with me."

Mary climbed down from the wagon and touched David on the arm as she walked toward Martha. She followed Martha into the house.

David unharnessed the horses and led them into the corral. The horses went immediately to the watering trough for a drink. David went into the stable and got a bale of hay, then spread it out for the horses to eat. As soon as he had the horses taken care of, he walked to the house and knocked on the door.

Martha came to the door and let David in. The first thing he saw was a big man sitting on a chair with his leg propped up on a footstool. The leg had two splints on either side tied in place with pieces of cloth. There was little doubt that he would be unable to do the work required of a blacksmith.

"Come in, young man. My wife tells me you are a blacksmith," he said as he pointed to a chair.

"Yes, sir," David replied as he sat down.

Stephen and David talked for the better part of an hour about blacksmithing. By the time they were finished, Stephen was convinced that David was a blacksmith, and he could run his blacksmith shop and livery stable until he was able to return to work.

"Well, son, I think I can leave my blacksmith shop in your hands until I'm able to return to work. I have a list of things that need to be made or repaired. If you have any problems you can come to me for help."

"I'm sure we can work together," David said with a smile.

"Are you two done talking about the shop? If you are, I think this young couple needs something to eat."

"Sounds good to me," Stephan said.

"Let me help you," Mary said with a grin.

The two women went into the kitchen and prepared a meal. After they finished the meal, David went out to the stable and took care of all the animals. He fed and watered them, and rubbed down his horses. He also shoed a horse that Stephan had not been able to do before his accident.

When it was time to turn in for the night, David and Mary were shown to a room in the house. In the room, there was only one bed. David looked at Mary and she looked at him. She smiled at him.

"I guess they think we are married. What should we do?" Mary asked.

"What do you want to do? We probably should tell them that we are not married."

"I saw a church in the center of town. Maybe we could go to the church and get married tomorrow," she suggested.

"What would you think of asking Martha and Stephan to stand up for us?"

"They seem like really nice people. Maybe we should tell them we are not married."

"Should we tell them now?" David asked.

"Yes. Not to tell them would be like telling a lie. I like them. I wouldn't want them to be angry with us, or even disappointed."

"Okay, I'll tell them. Then I'll go sleep in the barn."

"I'll go with you to tell them," Mary said.

David and Mary left the bedroom and went out into the kitchen where they found Stephan and Martha sitting at the table.

"Is there something wrong?" Martha asked.

"No, but we have something to tell you," David said then looked at Mary.

"What is it, son?" Stephan asked.

"Well, you see, Mary and I are not married."

Stephan and Martha looked at each other, then looked at David and Mary.

"Why didn't you say something before?"

David looked at Mary as if he was looking for an answer to Stephan's question.

"David and I ran away from my father. He refused to let us get married," Mary said.

"We are planning to get married the first chance we get. This is the first town we have come to since we ran away," David said.

"My father threatened to kill David if I ever saw him again. I love David and he loves me," Mary said excitedly. "My father has been very unreasonable. He doesn't like David because his family doesn't have much. His father is a blacksmith, and a very good one. David is also a very good blacksmith. He wants to start his own blacksmith shop someday. It may never make him rich, but it's good honest work," Mary said as if she was pleading their case.

Stephan looked from Mary to David. He had to admit that the young couple sitting at his table had courage, even if they didn't plan things well. Stephan looked at David for a moment.

"It will be at least a week before the preacher makes his rounds and comes to the church in the center of town," Stephan said. "What do you suggest in the meantime?"

David looked at Mary, then turned and looked at Stephan.

"I was thinking that Mary could sleep here in the house. I would sleep in the barn, or in the wagon. We have several quilts."

"That sounds like a reasonable arrangement," Martha said. "What do you think, Stephan?"

"I hate to have you sleeping in the barn, but it does sound like a reasonable solution, at least until the preacher comes."

"After the preacher comes and we get married, we can stay in the room together," Mary said. "At least until you can return to work."

"I think that will work," Stephan said.

Over the next few days, David worked hard to finish some of the projects Stephan had started before he broke his leg. David was able to do the work that needed to be done to make some of Stephan's customers happy. It seemed some of them had been waiting for over a week to get the item they had ordered to be made.

As time went by, David began to earn a reputation as a very good blacksmith. The town folks would stop by from time to time to thank him for helping Stephan out while he was unable to work.

Mary spent a lot of time helping Martha with the household chores, including cooking and cleaning as well as helping to care for Stephan. Mary soon proved herself to be very good at baking, which impressed Martha.

One day when the sun was shining, Stephan asked if someone would help him out to the shop. He said he wanted to watch David work and keep him company. The three of them got together and carried him outside and sat him down in the sun where he could watch David.

"How's it feel to get out of the house for a little while?" David asked after the women went back inside.

"It feels great. I hear from some of the town folks that you're doing a good job. I thought I'd come out and see for myself."

"Glad to have the company."

David and Stephan spent most of the day together. Stephan was beginning to look at David as more of a son, than someone who worked for him in his time of need.

Mary and Martha were working in the house when Martha walked by a window. She stopped and looked out toward the livery stable. She could see her husband and David. Although they were talking, she could see that David was still working on something.

"Stephan is talking to David as if he was his son," Martha said without thinking.

"What did you say?" Mary asked.

"Oh. I'm sorry. I was just thinking aloud."

"I thought you said that 'Stephan is talking to David as if he was his son'. Do you think he really feels that way about David?"

Martha looked a little embarrassed that Mary had heard her. She turned and looked at Mary.

"Yes, I believe he thinks of David like he would if David was his son. You see, we have not been able to have any children. Stephan had never been able to get close to any young people until you and David showed up. It was like a blessing to have someone like David come to help him," Martha said as tears came to her eyes.

Mary walked over to Martha and put her arms around her. She held Martha and let her have a moment to cry. When she was done, Mary stepped back.

"David is a very special man. That is why I love him so. He loves his work as a blacksmith and he loves me. My father couldn't see that in him."

"It's a shame your father couldn't see that the two of you are in love."

"Yes, it is. I don't think my father will ever under-stand," Mary said with a hint of sadness in her voice.

"Maybe he will come around some day."

Mary nodded as if she hoped Martha was right, but she had her doubts. Her father had always been very protective of her.

Several days had passed when Martha pulled Mary off to the side to speak to her alone. Martha asked Mary to come out to the kitchen.

"Mary, in a couple of days the preacher will be here. How would you like to wear my wedding dress? I think with just a couple of tucks here and there it would fit you."

"I would love to have a wedding dress, but are you sure you want me to wear yours?"

"Of course. It would be like having my daughter wearing it."

Over the next couple of days, Mary and Martha worked on the dress while David worked in the blacksmith shop and livery stable.

When the big day arrived, David was in the church with Stephan and the preacher. David had made crutches for Stephan so he could get around on his own. His leg was healing nicely, but he still couldn't put any weight on it. They were waiting for Martha and Mary to come to the church.

David was talking to the preacher when he heard a scream from Mary. David ran out of the church to find that Mary's father had her by the arm.

"Take your hands off her," David yelled at her father.

"I will not. She is going back home with me."

"I don't want to go with you," Mary screamed at her father.

Suddenly, there was the sound of a gunshot, followed by silence. Everybody stopped and turned to look toward the church. Standing on the front porch of the church and leaning on his crutches was Stephan with a pistol in one hand.

"You, mister, take your hands off that woman."

As Mr. Erickson looked at Stephan, he loosened his hold on Mary, but didn't let go of her. She jerked free and ran to David. When she got to David, she moved around behind him.

"I don't know who you are, but that is my daughter," Mr. Erickson said, the anger he was feeling showed in his voice.

"I am Stephan Jenkinson and these young people are like family to me. I protect my family. You look at your daughter like she is something you own, not like the young woman she is. You don't deserve to call her your daughter."

"My daughter is too young to marry someone like him," he said as he pointed at David. "She is returning to where she belongs, with her mother and me."

"I would really hate to shoot you on her wedding day, but I will if you even think about dragging her away from here. She has chosen her own life, and that is to marry this man and live with him," Stephan said sharply.

"He is nothing but a blacksmith's son. A man who will never amount to anything," Mr. Erickson said with a tone of distaste.

"That's where you're wrong, mister," a tall man said from the crowd that had gathered nearby. "That young man has more sand, and more skill to make things that are badly needed in this part of the country than most men."

"Who are you?" Mr. Erickson demanded.

"I'm the man who will throw you in jail if you so much as delay this wedding," he said as he pulled back his coat to reveal a marshal's badge.

"You can't do that. I have every right to take my daughter back home."

"Excuse me. Miss, but do you want to go with this man?" the marshal asked.

"No, I want to marry David and stay with him."

"Guess that settles it. She is going to marry this young man, and you, sir, will not try to stop it. If you don't leave this couple alone, I have a nice jail cell you can spend the next ten days in while you are waiting for the circuit judge.

Mary and David went inside the church while Mr. Erickson was left outside. Most of the town folks attended the wedding and cheered the newlyweds. That was all except Mr. Erickson. He was not allowed in the church for fear he would cause trouble and disrupt the wedding.

After the wedding, David and Mary stepped outside the church. Mr. Erickson was standing next to the hitching rail out in front of the church.

Mary was hanging onto David's arm for dear life. It was clear to everyone there that she was afraid of what her father might do. He had already threatened to kill David.

Mr. Erickson watched as his daughter walked out of the church. He looked at Mary as if he couldn't believe it. He had watched her marry David through the window of the church.

The town marshal had walked out of the church before the young couple to make sure Mr. Erickson didn't cause them any trouble.

He was standing only a few feet from Mr. Erickson.

"I don't care if she is married or not," Mr. Erickson said to the marshal. "She is going back with me, and I will see to it that she is not married to anyone as soon as we get home."

"She is not going with you, and you best get out of this town before I lock you up." The marshal said sharply.

David and Mary walked toward the marshal and stood close to him.

"Mr. Erickson, Mary and I don't want you to end up in jail, or to go home angry with us. We don't hold anything against you," David said hoping to get Mr. Erickson to be reasonable.

"All Mary and I want is to be happy together. We are happy here. Mr. and Mrs. Jenkinson have given me a chance to prove myself. I don't know if we will be happy here, but we think we will. We want to stay here among the people who have become our friends. You and Mrs. Erickson will be welcome to visit us anytime you want, but we are going to lead our own lives the way we want, just like you and Mrs. Erickson have done. That means we are going to stay here. I have a good job and Mrs. Jenkinson and Mary are going to open a bakery and café here," David said as Mary firmly hung onto his arm.

Mr. Erickson looked at David for a minute or two, then turned and looked at all the people who had been to their wedding. The whole town had turned out for the wedding. Looking back at his daughter, he was wondering if they were really going to be happy living in a small town on the prairie. He also realized that there was no way of knowing what the future would hold for them, or anyone else for that matter.

Mr. Erickson began to realize that even if he could force his daughter to return with him, he would lose her respect and her love. Mr. Erickson looked at David and at his daughter for a moment.

"I hope you can forgive me some day," Mr. Erickson conceded. "I really hope you are happy and you have a good life. I will tell your mother that I found you and that you are married and doing well. I will also tell her that you are happy here. It is time for me to go."

Mary let go of David's arm and walked up to her father. She reached out and put her arms around him.

"I am happy, Daddy," she said then kissed him on the cheek.

Mr. Erickson held his daughter for a moment, then let her go. He looked at David.

"Take care of her," he said to David, then stuck out his hand.

"I will, sir," David said as he took Mr. Erickson's hand and shook it.

"I'm sure you will. I best be leaving."

Mary and David bid Mr. Erickson goodbye, then stood there watching him leave.

Mary and David stayed in the small town and watched it grow. Mary and Martha opened the bakery and café. David continued to work with Stephan, then took over the blacksmith shop and livery stable when Stephan was unable to keep it going. After Stephan passed away, Martha and Mary continued to run the bakery and café together.

David and Mary raised a family, two sons and a daughter, and lived out their lives together in the little town on the prairie.

A LONG DAY ON FLAT ROCK

Robert Olson was laying quietly on his bedroll looking up at the clear blue sky. He was thinking it might be a good idea if he got up, had his breakfast then got on his way. A rather large buckskin horse was standing quietly only a couple of yards away from him. The horse looked like it was asleep. Just as Robert sat up, his horse turned and looked at him.

"You ready to get on the trail again? We can't be more than about ten or twelve miles southwest of Deadwood."

Robert stood up and gathered a few branches of wood to build a small fire to cook his breakfast of bacon, coffee and biscuits. He was just about to strike a match to start the fire when he heard the report of a rifle. The shot came from only a short distance from where he was kneeling. Robert quickly blew out the match, stood up, grabbed his rifle and ran over toward the edge of a rocky outcropping only about ten yards away. He laid down on the flat rock, then crawled out to the edge.

At first, he didn't see anything in the small valley below. It wasn't until a second shot was fired that he saw the small cabin back in among the trees. He wasn't sure if the shot came from the cabin or from someplace close to the cabin.

He laid on the flat rocky outcropping and continued to watch. Nothing seemed to move. Robert had no idea if someone was hunting near the cabin, or if someone was defending the cabin, or if someone was attacking someone in the cabin. If someone was defending the cabin, he could not see anyone around. The forest was fairly thick making it hard to see if anyone was near the cabin.

Robert got up and ran to his saddle that laid on the ground where he had been sleeping just moments ago. He opened his saddle bags and retrieved his field glasses then returned to the edge of the outcropping. As soon as he was lying down at the edge of the outcropping, he began slowly scanning the area around the cabin. It took him several minutes before he saw movement in among the trees near one corner of the cabin. Whoever it was, it looked like he was sneaking toward the cabin.

He watched what was going on for several minutes. Robert had no idea who the man was and why he was attacking the cabin. Whoever it was, he had no desire to get involved in a gunfight when he didn't know what was going on. Besides, he had not heard another shot for sometime. He decided it was none of his business.

He stood up and walked over to his bedroll and rolled it up. Robert saddled his horse and tied the saddlebags and bedroll to the saddle. Even with all his activity in getting ready to move out, he couldn't get the cabin out of his mind and what might be going on there. He was about to swing into the saddle when he heard a woman's voice.

"You're not takin' my cabin or my land," the woman yelled.

Hearing the woman yelling caught Robert's attention immediately. He wondered if she was all alone to defend her cabin and land. Maybe it was time to get involved. Attacking a woman went against almost everything Robert believed in. He took his rifle and ran back to the edge of the outcropping. Looking out over the edge, he saw a man standing very close to the cabin. Robert took a quick look around but could not see anyone else.

When he saw the man strike a match and light a torch, Robert couldn't let him burn down the cabin with a woman in it. He took careful aim and fired a shot at the man with the torch. His shot hit the corner of the cabin, only inches from the man's head, causing splinters of wood to hit the man in the face. The man dropped the torch and grabbed his face then stumbled back into the woods, out of sight.

Not knowing if there were others trying to get the cabin away from the woman; Robert ran to his horse, jumped in the saddle and rode away from his camp. After riding the short distance around the end of the flat rocky outcropping from where he had fired his gun, he stopped his horse. He got out of the saddle and tied the horse to a tree.

Walking slowly through the forest toward where the cabin was located, he was careful not to make any noise. He stopped suddenly when he heard voices.

"Where'd that shot come from?" a voice asked.

"Up atop that flat ledge overlookin' the cabin," a second voice replied.

"Any idea who it was?"

"Nope. Didn't see no one."

"Did you see how bad Frank was hit?"

"Nope, but I seen him crawlin' back inta the trees. I'd guess he was hurt some, but he made it ta cover."

"Ya know where George is?"

"Last I seen of him, he was workin' his way 'round to the other side of the cabin."

"Go find him and tell him to do nothing until we find out whose shootin' at us and where he's at. Then go see how Frank's doin'."

"Okay."

Robert heard someone moving through the woods. He was trying to be quiet, but not doing very well at it. From what was said, and what Robert had heard, there were four men trying to take the cabin away from the woman. There might have been more. For that matter, there might have been someone else in the cabin, but Robert didn't think so.

From where Robert was at the moment, he could see the back of the cabin was built up against a solid rock cliff that went up well above the roof of the cabin. The position of the cabin made it clear there were only three sides of the cabin exposed, which would make it easier to defend.

He continued to watch what was going on in the valley from his new position. Robert caught a glimpse of two men in among the trees. They seemed to be looking for someone. They were moving cautiously and looking up toward the outcropping often as if they expected to be shot at by someone on the top of the flat rock. It was obvious they were looking for Robert. Something else was obvious. They were not any of those he had seen before, and they had not come from where the two men had been talking. That bit of information added up to at least six men trying to take the cabin, although there may still be others.

When he no longer could see anyone, Robert decided it was time for him to get away from his present location. He returned to his horse and swung into the saddle then walked his horse further away from the cabin.

Once he was sure he was far enough away from the cabin that his horse would not be seen, he stepped out of the saddle, hobbled his horse in a small clearing then removed the saddle, hiding it in some brushes. He took his saddle bags off the saddle and swung them over his shoulder. With his rifle in one hand, he started to work his way back toward the cabin. It was rather slow going as the forest was fairly dense. The trees were not very close together, but there were a lot of bushes and undergrowth. He had to stay low to avoid being seen.

Robert stopped short when he saw eight horses tied to a rope hung between two trees. There was also a man standing near the horses and looking in the direction of the cabin. It looked as if he was standing guard to make sure no one stole the horses. If that was the case, he was looking in the wrong direction.

Robert began to move closer to the horses, using every bit of cover he could find. When he was only about twelve feet from the nearest horse, he heard someone call out. He ducked down behind a large bush and watched.

"You okay, Fred?" a voice called out.

"Yeah," the man guarding the horses replied.

"Keep an eye out. Someone took a shot at Frank. We don't know if he's alone. There might be more than one of 'um."

"I'll keep an eye out."

"If'n you see someone, make sure it ain't one of us 'for you shoot at him."

"I'll be careful," the guard answered.

The guard took a moment to look all around. Robert had crawled under a bush where he could not be seen. The guard turned back and looked toward the cabin.

Robert watched as the man walked away from the guard. Robert thought about what was going on. He wasn't sure, but he doubted it was lawmen trying to get the woman out of the cabin. Any of the lawmen he knew would try to talk her out of the cabin. From what he had heard so far, there hadn't been any sort of conversation between the woman and the men trying to burn her out.

There were just too many things Robert didn't know. He didn't know why the men wanted her out of the cabin, who the men were, and what they hoped to gain by getting the cabin.

He again looked at the cabin and studied it. The fact that it was up against the rocky cliff caused him to think on it a bit. There appeared to be only one door into the cabin. It occurred to him there might be a mine entrance into the cliff from inside the cabin.

As Robert thought about the cabin, he began to think the woman might be trapped in the cabin, unless there was some other way out. Thinking the woman might be trapped, he thought about how he could help her. The cabin was almost as good as a fort. It had been built with rather large logs and there was at least one window on each of the three sides. The only problem was it would be hard to cover all three sides of the cabin by one person, but two people could cover it much better.

Robert also knew it would be hard for him to help her very much if he had to fight from the woods. It would be fairly easy for them to split up and keep him busy while the others burned the cabin down. The only way to prevent that would be for him to get inside the cabin, but how was he going to do it? He thought about it for a moment before he came up with an idea.

Robert slowly worked his way closer to Fred who was guarding the horses. When he was close enough, he sprung to his feet and attacked the guard. Fred barely had time to see Robert before he was struck in the face with the butt of Robert's rifle. Fred went down without a sound, his nose and jaw broken. Robert looked at him for a moment to make sure that he was out of the fight.

With Fred out of the way, Robert untied the horses from the rope one at a time then tied them loosely together using their reins. Once he had them tied together, he slowly moved closer to the cabin while leading the horses. When he was only a few yards from the cabin, he yelled and smacked the lead horse on the rear to get the horses to run in front of the cabin. As the horses ran past the cabin, he ran beside them as fast as he could, using the horses for cover. When he got to the door of the cabin, he turned and slammed his shoulder into the door. The door flew open and he fell on the floor inside the cabin. He quickly kicked the door closed.

As soon as the horses were past the door to the cabin, shots began to ring out, some of them hitting the door and door frame. Robert rolled over and looked up only to find the woman pointing a rifle at him. Robert quickly dropped his rifle and put his hands out where she could see them.

"Don't shoot. I came to help you."

"How do I know that," the woman said, her voice showing her anger at those trying to take her cabin.

"I guess you don't, but I'm here. Did you hear the shot that hit the corner of your cabin? There was a man with a torch who was ready to burn your cabin down. I'm the one who fired the shot that stopped him."

"I heard the shot and saw someone up on the outcropping on the other side of the draw."

"Yes, ma'am. I was the one on that big flat rock," Robert said.

"Well, don't just lay there. We have a cabin to defend," she said.

"Yes, Ma'am," he said as he smiled at her and stood up.

Robert quickly picked up his rifle and moved to one of the windows on the side of the cabin while the woman moved to the other side. He saw one of the men outside dodging between trees while trying to move closer to the cabin. Robert took careful aim and fired. The man slumped over and fell to the ground.

Robert quickly moved to the window on the front of the cabin. Standing next to the window he looked out in time to see another man attempting to move in closer. The man was in a position where he could be seen from the side window better than from the front window. A shot was fired from the side window and the man dropped his gun, grabbed his arm and ran back in among the trees.

Robert smiled as he looked across the room at the woman. She smiled back at him.

"What's your name," Robert asked as he turned his attention to the outside.

"Martha, Martha Carlson."

"You wouldn't happen to be Captain Jack Carlson's wife? If I remember, he had a wife named Martha."

"Yes. Did you know Jack?"

"Yes. I was his sergeant at the Battle of Shiloh in 1862. He was injured there and I lost track of him."

"What's your name?"

"Robert Olson."

"I heard about you. Jack spoke well of you. Jack and I moved out here after he recovered, homesteaded this place, and discovered gold in this cliff. We built the house in front of the mine so no one would know about it."

"It looks like someone found out," Robert said.

"Yeah, it sure does. They killed Jack about a week ago when he was in town for supplies."

"I'm sorry to hear that. He was a good man."

"Yes, he was. The leader of the men out there is Tom Ray, a local bully and gunfighter."

"I've heard of him," Robert said as he watched a couple of men moving among the trees. "Any idea who is with him?"

"Probably his three brothers."

"There are at least four others. There were eight saddle horses tied out there before I ran 'um off," he said as he watched what was going on outside.

"Martha, can you see the man in the red shirt."

"Yeah, I can see him."

"Do you think you could hit him?"

"Maybe."

"Shoot him."

There was dead silence in the cabin for almost a minute before a shot rang out. Robert could see the man as he fell to the ground and grabbed his knee. Martha's shot had hit him in the knee, smashing it and taking him out of the fight.

Martha's shot almost immediately drew a response. There was a volley of shots with the bullets hitting the cabin in and around the window. Martha ducked down and grabbed her arm. A splinter of wood from the window frame had hit her.

Robert didn't immediately see that Martha had been injured. He was busy returning fire. He hit one of those firing at the cabin.

As soon as the shooting stopped he looked over at Martha. She was sitting on the floor beneath the window holding her arm. He quickly ran to her side.

Robert knelt down in front of her. He could see the blood on the sleeve of her blouse. He tore her sleeve open then quickly wrapped her arm with his bandana to stop the bleeding. Robert quickly stood up and turned toward the window. He fired a shot at one of the men to let him know that the fight was still on. He then quickly ran to the other window and fired a shot into a bush where he had seen one of the men hiding. As luck would have it, he actually hit the man, but didn't do any serious damage to him.

Robert looked across the room and saw Martha looking at him. Her expression was that of someone who didn't understand his actions. He didn't know what to say, but he thought he should say something.

"I just wanted them to know that we were both still in the fight," he said with a grin.

Martha smiled back at him then reached for a pistol that was lying on a table near the window. She then turned and peeked out the window. She was ready to continue the fight, but it was suddenly quiet. She listened for a few minutes before she looked at Robert.

"Do you think they left?" she asked.

"I don't know. We hurt them pretty bad. At least four, maybe five of them are injured. I would think that would take some of the fight out of them."

"What do we do?"

"We wait. We don't know how many of them are in any condition to fight. Those able to fight might be waiting for it to get dark."

"Do you really think they will continue with so many of them injured?"

"They're hard men. They don't give up easily. We just have to wait and see what they do."

Robert kicked back and sat in a chair near a window so he could see out. Martha sat across the room at one of the other windows to watch. He could see her rub her arm just above where she was injured. He was sure the pain from the injury was not very bad, but her arm was probably aching. At the very least, it was uncomfortable for her.

Time passed slowly as the sun went down behind the hills to the west. If Robert remembered correctly there would be an almost full moon tonight. He was sure it would take a while before the light from the moon would shine into the valley. They would have to be ready for almost anything.

"Should I light a fire? It could get pretty cold tonight," Martha asked.

"No. Any kind of light in here would make it easier for them to see in and harder for us to see them."

"I hadn't thought about that," she said. "What about supper? I'm sure you haven't eaten since this morning."

"I'll get by," Robert assured her. "We have to keep a close watch. There's no telling what they might do."

Once again the cabin was silent. The only thing that disturbed the silence was the sudden sound of an owl hooting, but it was some distance from the cabin. Even that ended quickly and there was silence again. The night air was cool and there was a gentle breeze. The breeze was not enough to cause the pine trees to move. If anything moved outside the cabin, it would have to be either the men who attacked the cabin, or some animal moving in among the trees. With so many men around, there was not likely to be many animals that would hang around the area.

As the night went on, the moon crept over the hills and began to spread its light over the valley. Robert moved up close to the window and looked out. He carefully scanned the area looking for any sign of the attackers. While looking for anyone who might still be around, he began to think about the cabin being built so close to the rocky cliff and the entrance to the mine. He turned and looked at Martha.

"You said there is a mine here. Is the entrance to the mine behind that cabinet?" he asked in a whisper.

"Yes."

"How far back does it go?"

"About a hundred feet or so, maybe a might bit more."

"Is it straight back?"

"No. It goes back probably eighty to ninety feet then makes a sharp turn to the left. What are you thinking?" she asked.

"Is there any other way in or out of the mine?"

"Not really. There is a place that leads to the outside, but it's pretty small. It's hard to get to because it goes almost straight up and is too small for us to crawl through. You can't see out it, but Jack was sure it goes to the outside. We don't know where it comes out, but there is a slight draft that goes from here to the outside. What's on your mind?"

"I was just thinking. If we have to desert the cabin for some reason, the mine might be the safest place for us to go."

"Do you think we will lose the cabin?" Martha said with a hint of sadness in her voice.

"I hope not. I'm just trying to plan for what might happen."

Nothing was said for some time. The night continued to remain silent. Robert was wondering what would happen when the morning light started to fill the sky. With a little of the moonlight shining in the window, he could see that Martha had dozed off. He was sure the stress of the long day had finally caught up with her.

He turned and looked out into the darkness. He wasn't really expecting to see anything. It was a surprise when he saw what looked like the flash of a match being lit. He took careful aim at the place where he saw the light and fired.

The report of his rifle firing was quickly followed by the loud explosion of a stick of dynamite. When the sound of the explosion dissipated, the only sounds left were the cries of pain from a couple of men. It was clear they had decided to blow up the cabin, but Robert's shot had ended that idea.

As soon as the sound of the explosion had faded away, it was quiet again except for a few cries of pain that came from where the explosion had taken place. Robert could hear what sounded like a couple of men moving around in the darkness, but none of the sounds indicated that anyone was coming closer to the cabin. After a short time, it once again became deathly quiet. Martha and Robert kept watch for the rest of the night.

When morning came, they scanned the area but didn't see anyone. They waited and watched, but nothing happened for several hours.

"Do you think they've gone?" Martha asked.

"I don't know, but if that explosion killed or injured more than two of them I think they would have left. There's only one way to find out."

"Are you going outside?"

"Yes. Keep an eye out for anyone out there."

"Are you sure that's a good idea?"

"No, but I think it's the only way to find out if they've gone."

"Okay," she said.

Robert set his rifle next to the door, then drew his pistol. He glanced toward Martha before he reached out and opened the door. He looked out but didn't see anything. With his gun gripped firmly in his hand, he stepped outside and took a quick look around. Nothing moved. He ran into the woods in front of the cabin and carefully moved from tree to tree. It wasn't but a few minutes before he found the dead bodies of two men where the dynamite had exploded.

He continued to search the area. Robert found a total of four men dead. He was sure that there were at least two others who had been injured, but he didn't know how seriously they were injured. He also found only four horses.

Robert went and got his horse then led it and the other four horses to the cabin. He put the horses in a small corral just a few yards from the cabin. After talking to Martha, he loaded the four men on their horses and took them to Deadwood where he turned them over to the sheriff.

Robert took a little time to tell the sheriff what had happened, and who the men were who had tried to take Martha's cabin and land from her. When he finished talking to the sheriff, Robert returned to the cabin in the woods.

A month later, the sheriff stopped by to tell them he had caught three of the remaining men who had attacked Martha's cabin. He also told them that the fourth man died of his wounds.

Robert worked with Martha until winter came on. They got along very well, so he stayed on. Once winter had gone and spring came to the cabin, they rode into Deadwood and got married. They lived out their lives together in the little valley.

REVENGE FOR A HANGING

Ruth Cupper stood just outside the front door of the cabin looking out across the valley toward the ridge off to the east. As each moment passed, she became more concerned with the lateness of the hour. Her husband, Joseph, should have returned home hours ago, and she was getting worried. All she could think about was it had never taken him so long to go to the mercantile store at Silver City to pick up a few supplies.

She had to know what was keeping him. Had he run into some kind of trouble, was he injured, did his horse go lame? All sorts of reasons for his delay in getting home ran through her mind, but they did nothing to help her know why he was so late. She grew more and more impatient as time went by. She couldn't wait any longer.

Ruth dressed in pants and shirt, took the pistol in a holster off the peg by the door and put it on, then picked up a rifle and went out to the barn to saddle a horse. As soon as it was ready, she swung into the saddle and headed for the small town of Silver City. It was not a long ride. In fact, it was just on the other side of the ridge about eight or nine miles away. As she rode along a narrow wagon trail, she kept a close watch out for her husband, hoping that she would see him coming toward her.

Ruth had gone about six miles along the wagon trail that wound its way to the top of the ridge. As the sun was beginning to set, she reached the top of the ridge where she saw something hanging from the branch of a large tree just off to the side of the trail.

At first, she thought it was the carcass of a deer someone had shot and hung on the tree to butcher. But as she got closer, she realized it was a man who was hanging from the tree. She carefully moved closer. When she was only about twenty feet from the tree, she realized it was Joseph. She hurried the last few feet to the tree. As she moved up close to him, she knew he was dead.

Still in a state of shock, she just sat on her horse looking at him. It quickly became clear that he had been beaten and then hung from the tree. She found it hard to believe that it was really Joseph.

Tears began to come to her eyes as she stepped out of the saddle and walked up to the tree. Ruth untied the rope and slowly lowered Joseph to the ground. She took the rope from around his neck then sat on the ground and held his head in her lap as she cried.

After sitting with him for over an hour, she wiped the tears from her face and stood up. She had not realized that it had turned dark and the moon had started to rise over the hills to the east. Ruth took the bedroll off her saddle and wrapped Joseph in it. It was a struggle for her, but she finally managed to get him over the saddle. Once he was over her saddle, it occurred to her that she had not seen his horse. She looked around, but in the dark she didn't see the animal anywhere. Her first thought was whoever it was who hung her husband, had also taken his horse.

Not knowing what else to do, Ruth took hold of the reins of her horse and started walking toward the town of Silver City. The long walk gave her time to think about what she would do.

It was late when she arrived in front of the saloon. Across the street was the mercantile store and it was dark. She knew the owner of the mercantile store was also an undertaker and that he lived in the back of the store. She led her horse to the other side of the street and tied it to the hitching rail in front of the store.

She walked around to the backdoor of the store and pounded on the door. It took a couple of minutes before the light from a lantern showed in a window and it was only a minute or so after that before Mr. Summers came to the door. He was wearing his nightshirt.

"What is it? Oh, it's you, Mrs. Cupper."

"Yes."

"Where is Joseph?" he asked as he looked around expecting to see him.

"He's out in front."

"What's wrong?" he asked when he realized that she had been crying.

"Someone hung Joseph from a tree up on the ridge," she said then started to cry.

Mr. Summers couldn't believe what he had heard. He took her hand and led her into his living quarters. He had her sit down at the kitchen table.

"I'll be right back," Mr. Summers said then went into his bedroom to get dressed.

After returning to the kitchen, he waited for a few seconds while he looked at Ruth. She was still sitting on a chair at the kitchen table. He turned and left his living quarters. Mr. Summers walked around to the front of the mercantile store and found a horse with a body wrapped in a bedroll lying over the saddle. He untied the horse and led it around to the small barn behind the store. He led the horse into the barn, then took Joseph off the horse.

Since Mr. Summers was also the undertaker, he had several coffins in the barn. He placed Joseph in one of the coffins. One look told him that he had been beaten before he was hung. He laid the lid over the coffin, but did not nail it shut. He quickly returned to his living quarters and sat down across the table from Mrs. Cupper.

"I know this is a hard time for you, but do you know what happened?"

"No. When he didn't come home from coming here, I got worried. I followed the road and found him hanging from a tree," she said, then broke down and cried again.

Mr. Summers got up and made a pot of coffee while Ruth tried to regain her composure. It wasn't very long before the coffee was ready and it looked like Ruth was ready to talk again. Mr. Summers poured two cups of coffee and set them on the table. He sat down across from her.

She looked up at him, then at the cup. Ruth took a sip of the coffee then looked at Mr. Summers again.

"I didn't see Joseph's horse. If he was on his way home, he would have had our supplies on the horse. Did he get here at all?"

"No. I haven't see Joseph for three or four weeks. I was thinking just the other day that he should be along any day now."

"So, he never made it to your store?"

"No. Whoever did this to Joseph must have robbed him, too," Mr. Summers said thoughtfully. "You know, I saw two men come into town. One of them was riding a horse while leading a second horse that looked like it was lame. I didn't think much of it at the time, but the horse he was riding looked a little like Joseph's horse. I remember 'cause it seemed a bit strange since all three horses had saddles on them."

"You think the man's horse came up lame; and when Joseph came by, they killed Joseph and stole his horse?"

"I don't know, but it could have been," Mr. Summers said. "I know this much, they left the lame horse with the blacksmith, you know, Jake Smith."

"Have they left town?"

"I'm sure they did."

"I need to talk to Mr. Smith."

"I think you should wait for morning. We'll get Joseph buried, then talk to Jake. You can stay here for tonight. You can sleep on the sofa. You're so tired, you need to rest."

"Thank you, but - - -."

"You need to rest," he insisted. "I'll get you a blanket. There's nothing you can do tonight."

"I guess you're right," she conceded.

Mr. Summers got a blanket for her and helped her get settled on the sofa. As soon as she was resting, he blew out the lamp and went to his room. He laid in bed and could hear her crying in the darkness. It took a long time before he could no longer hear her. Hoping she had not done some-thing foolish like get up and leave, he looked in on her. She was still there and sleeping soundly. It had been a long hard day for her, he thought, then returned to bed.

When morning came, Mr. Summers was up and making breakfast as Ruth came into the kitchen. She looked a little better. Mr. Summers was sure that she did get at least some rest.

"Sit down. We'll have breakfast then take care of Joseph."

Ruth didn't say anything, she simply sat down at the table. It was only a few minutes before Mr. Summers put breakfast on the table.

"I'm sure you would like to have a few minutes before we take Joseph to the cemetery. I have a couple of men who will carry him to his resting place."

"Thank you," was all Ruth said.

After breakfast, they went out to the barn. Mr. Summers took the lid off the coffin, then stepped outside.

Ruth moved up to the coffin and looked at her husband. With tears in her eyes she spoke softly to him.

"I will not let them get away with this. I will find those who did this and they will pay for it."

Ruth turned and stepped outside the barn. She just looked at Mr. Summers and the other two men standing next to him. Ruth waited outside the barn while the men went inside to close the coffin. She was startled when she heard the hammer hit the first nail that secured the coffin lid in place. Each time the hammer hit a nail, she flinched. It wasn't long and the two men came out of the barn carrying the coffin with Mr. Summers right behind them. Ruth walked up next to Mr. Summers and walked beside him to the cemetery.

The small cemetery was only a short distance from Mr. Summers' mercantile store. The first thing Ruth noticed was the grave had been dug and was waiting for them. The two men set the coffin down over two ropes, then took hold of the ropes and lifted the coffin. They lowered it into the hole then pulled the ropes out of the grave. Mr. Summers said a few words about Joseph over the grave, then looked at Ruth.

Ruth was looking into the grave at the coffin, but said nothing. As soon as Mr. Summers had finished saying a few words from the Good Book, Ruth turned and started back to the barn where her horse had been stabled for the night. As she walked away, she could hear the sound of dirt being shoveled into the grave and landing on top of the coffin.

When she got to the barn, she saddled her horse. Taking the bedroll from the lame horse's saddle, she tied it to her saddle, then led her horse out of the barn. She swung into the saddle and rode down the street to the livery stable. She arrived just as the blacksmith arrived.

"Mr. Smith, did you see my husband's horse yesterday?"

"I don't think so. I saw a horse that looked a little like your husband's horse."

"It was Joseph's horse. Two men came in here with three horses. They murdered Joseph and stole his horse. Do you know where they went?"

"I have the lame horse here. I have the saddle, too. The horse will be fine in a few days," Sam said, not sure what he should say.

"Do you know where they were going?" she said rather sharply insisting on an answer.

"Ruth, you're not going after them, are you?"

"Yes. They killed Joseph and stole his horse. Yes, I'm going after them. Which way did they go?" she asked, demanding an answer.

Mr. Smith looked at her for a moment. He could see the determination in her eyes, and hear it in her voice.

"They went west out of here. They didn't say where they were going," he said reluctantly.

"Are you sure?"

"The only thing they said was they were going west. They didn't say why or where."

"Thank you," Ruth said then turned her horse and started after them.

Ruth headed west on the trail that took her out of the valley where Silver City was located to the narrow road that wound back into the hills. Ruth didn't care where the road went, she was on a mission, and that mission was to find and kill the men who hung her husband. She had no idea what they looked like, but she would know her husband's horse.

It didn't take her long to pick up the trail of her husband's horse. The animal had a very distinctive gait which left a distinctive hoofprint in the dirt.

It wasn't long before she found the place where they had camped for the night. She swung out of the saddle and looked over the area. She knelt down and tested the fire. Some of the coals from the fire were still a little warm. Judging from the warmth of the fire, and looking up at the sky, she was sure that she was no more than a few hours behind them. That bit of information told her they were not expecting anyone to be following them. She returned to the saddle and started following the trail left by them.

The sun was high in the sky when she drew up at a small creek. She stepped out of the saddle and led her horse up to the creek for a drink of water. She also took time to get a drink from the creek.

As she knelt by the creek, she looked off in the direction of the trail. Ruth wondered how far ahead of her they might be. From the look of the tracks, they didn't seem to be in any hurry.

From the looks of their tracks through the creek, she was gaining on them. She knew she would have to be careful so they didn't see her before she saw them.

Ruth waited a few minutes to give her horse a chance to eat a little of the grass at the edge of the creek. When the animal looked like it was done, she swung into the saddle and coaxed him forward into the creek. Her horse waded across the creek and up the short bank on the other side. Once on the other side, she nudged him along at a fairly fast walk.

Ruth kept a close watch on the tracks being left by the horses she was following. Since they were easy to follow, she watched more for a change of pace or any other movement that might indicate that they had figured out they were being followed.

The sun was starting to set in the western sky when she thought she could smell smoke. She drew up and sat in the saddle as she smelled the air. The breeze was coming from out of the west. She turned her horse off the trail and into the woods. She stepped out of the saddle and stood next to her horse.

Ruth glanced up at her horse. He was looking toward the west. His ears were also pointed west and he seemed to be smelling the air. Her horse had smelled the same thing she had. Not sure what to do, she just stood there, looking and listening for anything that didn't seem right.

Time seemed to pass slowly. She noticed it was getting darker. The sun had dropped below a distant ridge. Ruth also noticed that the smell in the air had changed. There was the smell of fresh brewed coffee mixed with the smell of wood burning. She immediately knew that it was a campfire she was smelling.

Ruth led her horse back into a small area where it could graze. She hobbled the horse, then removed the saddle and bedroll and set it at the base of a big pine tree. As soon as she had the horse settled down, she removed her rifle from the saddle scabbard and checked it.

Once she was ready, she slowly began to move among the trees, working her way toward where she was sure the fire would be. She was not sure if whoever was at the fire were the men she was looking for, but she had to find out.

It wasn't long before she could see the glow of the fire in the trees. She continued to work her way among the trees to get closer.

As she moved closer to the fire, she first spotted the horses. It was not hard for her to identify Joseph's horse even though it was fairly dark. She instantly knew she had found the two men she had been trailing.

Seeing Joseph's horse made her suddenly realize she had not made any plans on what to do when she caught up with them. Ruth knew she wanted them to pay for killing her husband, and that she wanted to see justice done. The one thing she had failed to do was plan how she was going to get justice for the death of her husband when she finally caught up to them.

To get justice in the true sense of the word would require her to capture them and turn them over to the law. The closest lawman was in Hill City. How was she going to do that without getting herself injured or possibly killed?

Maybe it was time to just kill them, she thought. No one would know the difference out here, or even care. The vision in her mind of seeing her husband hanging from the tree was all it took for her to realize that they deserved nothing better. It also made her angry enough to want them dead. With it set clearly in her mind what she was going to do, she began to plan how she was going to do it.

Being as careful as she could, she slowly worked her way closer to their fire. It wasn't long and she was where she could see them clearly. She could even hear them talking in the stillness of the night.

"What do you think that guy's wife will do when she finds out we hung her man?" the smaller of the two men asked.

"Ah, she's like most women. She'll cry, and when she's all cried out, she'll report it to the law. By that time, we'll be in Wyoming Territory where they can't touch us."

"You really think so?"

"Yeah. Women don't have the strength or the nerve to go after a man, except when she's lookin' for a man to take care of her," the bigger man said with a laugh.

"Yeah. When they go after a man, they can turn on the charm; but they ain't got the stomach to shoot a man."

The more they talked the angrier Ruth got. She would show them what an angry woman could do. She slowly moved around a rock that gave her a better view of the two men at the campfire. Once she was in position, she leveled her rifle at the campfire right in front of the bigger of the two men. Just as he reached for the coffee pot on the fire, she pulled the trigger. The bullet hit the campfire scattering burning sticks of wood and coals all over. She then quickly fired a second shot that hit the little man square in the chest dropping him over backwards.

The bigger man drew his pistol and tried to see where the shots had come from, but it was hard for him to see with ashes in his face and eyes. He blindly fired a couple of shots in the general direction of where he thought the shots had come from, then dropped down on the ground. He laid on the ground for a few minutes listening for some noise that would hopefully let him know where the shooter was located. Not hearing anything, he started to crawl away from the fire in the hope of finding cover in the trees. The silence soon made him become impatient.

"Who's out there," he called out.

Ruth could hear the fear in his voice. She could also see him trying to look around while trying to clear his eyes of the ash.

"Where are you?" he called out.

Ruth took careful aim at the ground right in front of him. She slowly pulled the trigger. There was a loud bang from the rifle then a shower of dirt, pieces of small rock and pine needle raining over the big man.

The big man screamed as dirt kicked up hitting him. He covered his head.

"Who are you?" he shouted still not able to see who or where his attacker was hiding.

He suddenly heard something behind him. In his fearful state, he could not identify the sound. He swung around, sat up, then fired a shot at the shadow of someone he thought he saw, but it was only a tree.

He never heard Ruth move up behind him. He felt a sharp pain in his arm when it was struck by Ruth's rifle. He dropped the gun and grabbed his arm. As he did, Ruth dropped a rope over his head and pulled it tight. He reached up and grabbed at the rope to keep it from strangling him.

"How does it feel to have a rope around your neck?" Ruth asked.

"Who are you?" he asked, but his words came out strained with the rope so tight around his neck.

"I am the wife of the man you hung from a tree then stole his horse. I'm the woman who you don't think has the strength or the nerve to come after you. And I am the woman who killed your partner and will hang you like you did my husband."

Being very careful not to let him get any slack in the rope, she backed up a little way away from him. He had his fingers of both hands in the rope in an effort to keep it was strangling him.

Ruth tossed the end of the rope over a large branch of a big pine tree, then began to pull it tight. The big man rolled over and crawled toward the tree in his effort to keep it from strangling him as she pulled up the slack in the rope.

"Stand up," she said, still holding the end of the rope.

"No. I'm not going to let you hang me," he said with fear in his voice.

Ruth looked at him for a moment then tugged on the rope. When he still didn't stand up, she tugged on it harder.

"Get up," she demanded as she tugged on the rope.

"No," he said.

The rope was getting too tight and he was finding it hard to breathe. He could not resist any longer. He stood up. As soon as he stood up, Ruth pulled the slack out of the rope so he was almost standing on his tiptoes. She tied the end of the rope to another branch.

"I would suggest you not move too much. If you do, you might slip and hang yourself."

Ruth turned and walked into the darkness.

"You're not leaving me like this?"

Ruth did not answer him. She walked out and got her horse then brought the animal closer to the fire. She thought she saw a sign of relief from the big man's face, but it quickly disappeared when he saw the horse.

Ruth took a piggin' string from her saddle bag and walked up behind the big man. She grabbed his arm, but he resisted.

"You put your hands behind your back or I'll kick your legs out from under you and hang you right there."

The big man put his hands behind his back knowing he really didn't have a choice. She tied his hands together then gave the rope just enough slack that it allowed him to stand flat on his feet, but that was all. After he was secured, Ruth got out her bedroll and laid it down. She gathered up all the guns from the two men and then laid down with her back against a big tree while holding a pistol in her hand. It took her a while to relax enough to allow her to sleep.

When morning came, she woke and looked over at the tree. The big man was still there, his hands behind his back and the rope still securely around his neck. She smiled to herself. She was hungry, but didn't want to be around him any longer than necessary.

She wrapped the smaller man in his bedroll and put him over the back of his horse. She moved her husband's horse up next to the big rock that the big man could step up on. She untied the rope from the tree.

"Move over to the rock over there. If there's any slack in this rope, I will pull it so tight it will snap your neck. You climb up on that rock and get on the horse. One move I don't like and I'll hang you right here."

The big man did as he was told even though he was afraid that she was about to hang him. Once he was on the horse, Ruth took the reins of the horse and led it to the other. She took the end of the rope and looped it through the saddle under the saddle horn, then held the end as she got in the saddle of her horse.

"I suggest you don't do anything to make my horse or the horse you're on nervous. If you do, you are very likely to be hung while they drag you over the rough ground."

Ruth headed back to Silver City. It took her all day. A crowd gathered as she rode into town with a body hung over a saddle on one horse, and a man tied to the saddle with a rope around his neck on another horse.

"What ya got there," Mr. Smith asked.

"The men who hung Joseph."

"We'll take care of them from here," Mr. Smith said as he reached up and pulled the big man off the saddle. "We'll hang this one proper like. You want to be here when we do?"

"No. Right now, I want to get something to eat and get some rest, then go home."

Ruth went over to Molly's boarding house and got a good meal, then took a room where she laid down on the bed and cried until she fell asleep. She slept through the night.

The town had a quick trial that very day, while Ruth slept in the boarding house. That very evening, they hung the big man from a tree behind the livery stable. By morning, the two men had already been buried.

When Ruth got up, she went into the kitchen of Molly's boarding house for breakfast. She was met by Mr. Summers and Mr. Smith. They told her about the trial and that they had hung the man.

When she finished eating and was ready to leave the boarding house, she walked to the livery stable. She saddled her horse then rode out of town leading Joseph's horse.

Ruth returned to her small ranch on the other side of the ridge. She continued to work the ranch with the help of a hired hand. She married the hired hand a few years later and raised a family on the ranch.

THE PINKERTON DETECTIVE

A lone man rode into the town of Deadwood on a cold and rainy day. He sat tall in the saddle as his horse walked along the main street of town. He took his time as he looked from one building to the next. He didn't stop until he reined up in front of the sheriff's office. He sat in the saddle for a moment while he looked around.

The street was almost empty of any people, and there were only two or three horses tied to hitching rails. The man noticed the horses were tied in front of saloons. He grinned at the thought of men spending time in warm and dry saloons while their horses stood outside in the rain. He almost wished that he had been in a saloon rather than spending most of the day riding in the rain.

Suddenly, the door to the sheriff's office opened causing the man to turn and look toward the office. A tall man with a handle bar mustache and long hair that flowed out from under his cowboy hat stepped out onto the boardwalk.

"Well, it's about time you got here, Charlie. I wasn't sure the Pinkerton Detective Agency would let you loose to help a small town sheriff."

"You're lucky I got here at all. I was almost half way across the territory when I got word you needed some help. I wired my boss from a train station. He told me to help you anyway I can, since I was already out this way," Charlie said, then stepped out of the saddle and tied his horse to the hitching rail.

"Come on inside and get out of the rain."

Charlie stepped up on the boardwalk and shook the sheriff's hand.

"How the hell are you, Bill? It's been a long time."

"I'm doing okay, and it has been a long time. Come on inside, the coffee pot's on," Bill said.

Bill turned and went inside the sheriff's office. Charlie followed him. Once inside, Charlie removed his slicker and hung it over the back of a chair. He shook the water off his cowboy hat then set it on a chair. He then sat down while Bill got them both a cup of coffee. Once they had their coffee, Charlie held the cup in both hands and took a sip of the hot coffee, then looked at Bill.

"Your letter didn't say much. It just said that you needed help. How can I help you?"

"Someone is killing prospectors. There's been four prospectors murdered over just the past four weeks, the last one just a few days ago."

"You got any idea why they're being murdered?"

"My deputy and I first thought it was to steal their gold, but that doesn't seem to be the case. At least three of the four killed this past month still had their gold."

"Was their gold hidden well?"

"That's just it, their gold was easy to find. A kid could have found it. In one case, the prospector's gold was in a glass jar on a shelf above the head of his bed. It was easy to see," Bill said.

"Do you think the gold in the glass jar might have been a decoy to make others believe that it was all the gold he had?"

"I guess I hadn't thought about that, but it could have been."

"You said there were four in the last four weeks, were there any before that?"

"Yes. There were four last month, too. What are you thinking?"

"If what you're saying is what I'm hearing, you have had one murder a week for the past eight weeks or so. Is that right?" Charlie asked.

"I hadn't thought of it that way, but it has been one a week for the past eight weeks. You're right."

"How about when they were killed? Were they killed on the same day of the week or two every other week? What I'm doing is looking for a pattern."

"Give me a minute to think," Bill said.

Charlie sat quietly sipping his coffee while Bill thought about it. It wasn't long before Bill must have thought of something.

"Ya know, it's possible. Not all the bodies were discovered the day they were killed, but thinking back on it, it was possible they were all killed on the same day of the week."

"Do you have some idea what day of the week it might have been?"

"Yeah. There's a good chance that they were most likely killed late Saturday night or early on Sunday morning. You got some idea what's happening?"

"No, not yet, but Sunday morning might make a little sense."

"How so?"

"If the prospectors here are like a good many of them in other places, they tend to spend Saturday night doing a lot of drinking. They would most likely sleep pretty sound once they turned in."

"I see what you mean," Bill said thoughtfully. "A good many of them do come into town and tie one on Saturday night."

"Was there anything unusual about the camps of the prospectors? Possibly something that they all had in common?"

"I don't know of anything else they might have had in common. They were all typical prospectors. They all lived in tents, but then most of the prospectors live in tents. They were all killed by having their throats cut, probably while they were sleeping because they were found in bed, and they were all fairly new to this area. None of them having been here for more than about six months," Bill said as if it had just come to him. "Do you think they were killed because they were new here?"

"It's possible, but it seems unlikely. If someone was upset with a bunch of newcomers, I would think they would have done something about it sooner. But still, we can't overlook it," Charlie said.

"What do we do now?"

"I would like to see the camps of the last three killed."

"Okay, but why only the last three?" Bill asked.

"Because they are the ones most likely to gives us a clue. I would like to go out there tomorrow to see the site of the last prospector killed first. Right now, I need to get some rest, a bath and a good meal. I've been in the saddle for a long time. I'm sure my horse would like a bit of a rest, too."

"Take your horse over to the livery stable and tell Sam I sent you and to send the bill to me," Bill said.

"Okay," Charlie said as he stood up.

"Susan's boarding house is just down the street. You can stay there. The beds are clean and you can get a bath there. By the way, she is a darn good cook," Bill said with a grin.

"Okay. I'll meet you here in the morning."

"Okay."

Charlie took his horse to the livery stable. He took his saddle bags and bedroll off the horse, then left his horse in the care of Sam. With his horse being cared for, Charlie walked over to the boarding house and got a room. After a good meal and a bath, he went to bed to get some much needed rest. He didn't fall asleep quickly as his mind was thinking about what was going on, and why the prospectors were being murdered, but he finally dozed off.

When morning came, Charlie shaved then went downstairs to the kitchen for his breakfast. Once he had finished eating, he walked down the street to the sheriff's office. He walked in and found Bill sitting at his desk looking over some wanted posters.

"Good morning, Charlie. Did you get a good night's sleep?"

"Yes, I did. That Miss Susan sure can cook. That was the best breakfast I've had in quite some time. You looking for a suspect in those wanted posters?"

"Not really. These came in on yesterday's stagecoach. I didn't have a chance to look them over to see if there might be a poster on someone who is hanging around here. What do you say we get going?" Bill said then set the posters down and stood up.

Bill took a rifle from the rack behind his desk then started for the door. Charlie followed him out. Bill and Charlie walked down the street to the livery stable. They saddled their horses, then rode out of town.

They rode along the road to a place just outside of the city limits where they turned off the road onto a narrow trail that led back into the woods. It was only a minute or so before they reached a creek. They crossed the creek then turned and moved along the trail that ran alongside of the creek.

Charlie kept a watch for any danger that might come their way while looking over those panning for gold at the edge of the creek. The first thing he noticed was the prospectors stopped what they were doing to see who was riding along the creek. They continued to watch Charlie and Bill until they were well past them before they returned to panning for gold. The prospectors seemed watchful of any strangers in the area. It was easy for Charlie to understand with all the murders.

Charlie also noticed that since the trail was close to the creek, the prospector's tents were on the other side of the trail. It seemed to Charlie that the tents were about fifty to sixty feet apart. He guessed it was because the prospector's claims were about that distance apart. They rode past twelve tents before Bill reined up and waited for Charlie to ride up next to him.

"This is the tent of the last one who was murdered," Bill said as he pointed at the tent.

Charlie stepped out of the saddle and handed the reins of his horse to Bill. He walked up to the front of the tent, untied the flap, pulled it open and looked inside. There was a fairly large wooden box at the foot of the bed, a cabinet made of an assortment of wooden boards, a bed with a couple of wool blankets on it, and a floor of shale rock neatly laid out. On top of the headboard of the bed was a shelf with a picture of a woman, several books, and a small glass jar that looked like it had gold in it. He was surprised to see it was still there, since the man had been murdered several days ago. In fact, he was surprised to see anything left in the tent at all.

He turned and looked at Bill before he went inside the tent. Bill tied the horses to a small tree in front of the tent. When Bill stuck his head in the tent, he found Charlie carefully checking each piece of slate that covered the floor inside the tent.

"What are you looking for?" Bill asked.

"A hiding place."

Charlie moved the bed and checked the floor there, but found nothing. It wasn't until he moved the large wood box that he found a piece of slate that didn't seem to fit as well as the others. He pulled it up and found a tin can neatly buried in the ground.

Charlie looked over his shoulder at Bill before he turned back to the tin can and pulled the cover off it. He was a bit surprised at what he found. Inside the can was gold. The can looked to be about the size of a one gallon can and was almost full of gold dust and gold nuggets of various sizes.

"I've got a feeling that this was what the killer was looking for. Based on what I know so far, the miner was probably killed because the killer had a pretty good idea of what was here," Charlie said.

"Why did he leave it?"

"My best guess was something had caused him to leave before he could finish searching for it."

"You think he will come back and try to find it later?"

"Probably, but he will wait 'til things cool down a bit."

"I would have to agree with you. The only question I have is were the others killed because someone thought they had found large amounts of gold?"

"I don't know, but it is certainly a possibility. My question is, why was this man killed and the gold not found? It makes we wonder if someone might have come by and the killer had to scramble out of here before he found it."

"You think it's possible that he was killed for some other reason than to steal his gold?"

"Let's look at the other tents," Charlie said without answering Bill.

Bill led Charlie to the tent of the next to the last man killed. When Charlie looked inside, he found it was not all that much different from the first tent expect that there was nothing left inside, and there was no shale on the floor. Charlie stood in front of the tent and looked down the row of tents. He was sure that everything in this tent had been taken by other prospectors. It was not uncommon for prospectors to be scavengers for things they could use to make their life a little more comfortable.

"I'm going back to the first tent. I would like you to check out the other tents from the victims to see if they are like this one," Charlie said.

"Sure," Bill said, then turned and walked down the row of tents.

Charlie went back to the first tent then walked around behind it. He looked at the ground behind the tent, then looked at the surroundings. He didn't expect to find any tracks because of all the rain lately. He did, however, see a man standing behind the row of tents watching him. Charlie decided to have a talk with him.

"You there. I would like to have a talk with you," Charlie said as he started toward the man.

The man took a quick look around, then suddenly took off running. He ran along behind a couple of the tents before he darted out to the trail.

Charlie took off after him. It didn't take him long to catch up to the old prospector. He grabbed the prospector. Just as he did, a several other prospectors came up from the creek. They had picks, shovels and clubs as they approached Charlie.

"Hey, what the hell you doin'? You let him go if'n you know what's good for ya," one of the prospectors yelled.

"I'm a Pinkerton Detective. I'm here to find out who has been killing the prospectors along this creek. Now back off."

"We don't believe ya," one of the prospectors said sharply.

"You better believe him. The first one of you who causes him any trouble will get his head cracked," Bill said.

They all turned to see who was behind them. They saw the sheriff with a gun in his hand.

"I suggest that you go about - - - ," Bill started to say but was interrupted by Charlie.

"I want you all to sit down. We're going to have a little talk."

"You heard him, sit," Bill said sharply.

The four who had tried to come to the old man's aid found themselves sitting on the ground wondering what was going to happen next. Charlie looked at each one of them and watched for their reaction.

"I want to have a talk with each one of you. I'll start with you," Charlie said as he pointed to the old man who had run from him. "The rest of you will remain here with the sheriff."

Charlie took the old man and walked him back to the tent of the last man murdered. He took him inside the tent.

"Sit down," Charlie said."

He watched the old man very closely. It was clear that the old man was nervous. The old man sat down on the wooden box.

"Tell me about the man who lived in this tent before he was murdered."

"What about him?"

"Did he have any enemies?"

"None I knows about."

"How was he doing as a prospector? Was he finding any gold?"

"He found a little color, but nothin' ta get excited 'bout. I don't think he was doin' any better than the rest of us, but most of us don't say too much to the others about what we find. We sort of keep it to ourselves."

"Do you know of anyone he might have had a problem with, or he didn't get along with?"

The old man looked like he might know of someone, but might be afraid to say.

"Talk to me. You know something, and I want to know what it is."

"If I talk ta ya, I won't be 'round long," the old man said.

"Who is it you're afraid of?"

The old man looked at Charlie for a few minutes. Charlie waited and watched the old man.

"I don't know his name, but they call him Gus. He's a big man. His tent is about five tents down from where the sheriff is now. He don't seem like the rest of us," the old man said, but didn't explain.

"What do you mean?"

"Well, he don't seem ta work as hard at prospectin' as the rest of us, but he seems ta have more gold than most of us. At least he spends a good amount of time in the saloons."

"Is it possible that Gus found a place where there is more gold?"

"I guess it's possible, but he don't seem ta work much. He's a lazy sort of fella. All he seems ta do is talk. He goes ta the saloon on Saturday night like most of us. He always seems ta have enough gold ta buy his drinks."

"Does Gus talk to anyone in the saloon?"

"He talks ta the other prospectors. Is that what you're wantin' ta know?"

"Does he talk to anyone else?" Charlie asked ignoring the old man's question.

"Nah. He don't talk ta no one else, 'cept the barkeep."

Charlie looked at the old man while he thought about what he had been told. He wondered if the barkeep and Gus had something to do with the robberies and murders.

"You thinkin' of somethin'," the old man asked.

"Yeah. You can go."

Charlie sat on the edge of the bed and watched the old man leave the tent. As soon as he was gone, he sat there just thinking. It was Saturday. He wondered if it might not be a good idea to spend a little time in the saloon that Gus goes to and just watch him for a while.

He turned and looked at the flap of the tent, then stood up and walked outside. Charlie returned to where the others were sitting. He talked to several of the other prospectors, taking them one at a time to the tent before talking to them. He asked them the same questions he had asked the old man. It seemed that the only thing he found out was that the prospectors who had been killed had been to the same saloon that the man called Gus would go to on Saturday night. He felt he had enough information that he could form a plan. When he finished talking to the prospectors, he returned to where they were sitting.

"Okay, you can go about your business now."

Charlie watched them get up and leave. He turned and looked at the sheriff.

"Let's go back to town."

"We're done here?" Bill asked.

"We are for now."

Charlie didn't say anything more until they got back to town and were sitting in the sheriff's office. It was then he told Bill about his plan to go to the saloon that the big man who calls himself Gus went to on Saturday night.

That evening Bill and Charlie watched as the miners drifted into town. As soon as they saw the big man, Bill pointed him out.

"That's Gus," Bill said.

As soon as Gus was inside the saloon, Bill and Charlie walked down the street to the saloon they saw him enter. They took their time. Once in the saloon they walked to a table where they sat down. They watched Gus while making it look like they were just friends talking over a drink.

Gus spent some time talking to the barkeep. They noticed that the barkeep glanced at them. It wasn't long before Gus sat down at a table with a couple of other prospectors. After a short time, one of the prospectors looked around then leaned close to Gus. Shortly after their secret talk, the prospector got up and left. He was soon followed by Gus.

"It's time," Charlie said as he stood up.

Bill didn't comment, he simply stood up and followed Charlie out of the saloon. Once outside Charlie turned and looked at Bill.

"We need to get to the tents along the creek. I think Gus is going to kill that prospector tonight. I don't think he will try it until the prospector is in bed and asleep," Charlie said.

"Come on. I'll show you a quicker way to get there."

Bill didn't wait for a response from Charlie, he simply took off at a run. It didn't take them very long to get to where most of the tents were located along the creek. Bill pointed to a place among some rocks just off the trail that ran along the creek.

"We need to wait here. I don't know which tent is the prospector's," Bill said.

"Look, there's the prospector."

"What now?"

"I'll follow the prospector. I want to wait in his tent with him. You watch for Gus."

"Okay."

"Don't let Gus see you. We have to catch him when he tries to kill the prospector."

"What happens if he doesn't go to the prospector's tent?"

"You watch him to see if he goes to someone else's tent. If he does, grab him before he can kill that one."

Charlie snuck across the road and followed the prospector, staying far enough back that he was not seen. As soon as the prospector entered his tent, Charlie moved up close to it, looked around to see if there was anyone who could see him, then quickly stepped inside the tent. Just as the prospector was turning around to see who had followed him into the tent, Charlie grabbed him and put his hand over the man's mouth.

"Don't say a word. I'm not going to hurt you. I'm here to save your life," Charlie whispered. "I'm going to let you go. Please don't say a word."

The man nodded that he understood. Charlie took his hand off the man's mouth and watched as he turned around.

"I remember you. You're that Pinkerton man," the man whispered.

"I want you to lay down on your bed, but with your head at the foot of the bed. Blow out your lantern as if you are going to bed. I'll be right over here," Charlie said.

The man nodded, then watched as Charlie moved over to a corner of the tent, took his pistol from his holster and sat down. Once the man had blown out the lantern, they waited.

Time passed slowly. The silence of the night filled the air. Suddenly, Charlie heard the snapping of a twig just outside the back of the tent. Then there was the sound of a knife cutting the canvas of the tent. It was done so slowly that it was very hard to hear. The full moon let in just enough light that Charlie could see who had come into the tent.

"Drop the knife," Charlie said.

Suddenly, the shadow of a man lunged at him. He was so close that Charlie didn't have a chance to fire at him, but he grabbed the man pushing him out of the tent. The man started to get up and run, but Bill was right there.

"Stop or I'll shoot," Bill called out.

The man didn't stop and Bill fired one round that caught the man in the back. He fell to the ground and didn't move. Charlie and Bill walked up to the man, keeping their guns on him. Bill knelt down and rolled the man over. They were surprised to discover that it wasn't Gus. It was the barkeep from the saloon.

"It wasn't Gus after all," Bill said as he looked up at Charlie.

"No. It wasn't me," a voice behind them said.

Bill and Charlie turned to look at who had spoken to them. Gus was standing only a short distance from them.

"Who are you?" Charlie asked.

"I'm Marshall Gus Northum. One of the territorial marshals. I've been trying to find out who was killing the prospectors for the past three weeks. I had just figured it out and was about to trap him when I discovered you were here looking into it. As soon as I saw that you had set a trap for him, I decided I would let you carry it out. I would just back you up."

"I'm sorry we thought you were the one doing the killing," Charlie said.

"No big thing. You got him. One more for the Pinkerton Agency," he said with a grin.

"No. You can have the credit for this one."

After they put the body of the barkeep over the back of a horse, they returned to town. Bill took the body to the undertaker, then joined Charlie and Gus for a drink in the saloon. Shortly after their drink, they called it a night.

The next morning, the three men had breakfast together at Susan's boarding house. While at breakfast, Gus explained what had been going on.

"The barkeep would watch the prospectors when they came in on Saturday night. He would see who seemed to have a good supply of gold. After making sure they had enough to drink, he would find out where their tent was located. When it got late and he closed up, he would go out, kill his victim then search their tent for the gold," Gus said.

"Why didn't he take the gold in the last man's tent? It set on the shelf above the bed," Bill asked.

"It was a decoy, just as you suggested. He knew the prospector had found more than what was on the shelf," Charlie said.

"How did he know?" Bill asked.

"A lot of men tend to talk too much when they've had a few too many drinks. It was easy to get the men to talk to the barkeep," Gus said.

"I see. Well, I'm glad this is over," Bill said. "I want to thank both of you for helping me on this."

"No problem. It's always good to help each other," Charlie said.

After breakfast, they said goodbye to each other and went on their way. Charlie went east to his next assignment in Pierre, Gus went on north to Sturgis to investigate claims of cattle rustling, and Bill returned to the routine of keeping the town of Deadwood safe.

HUNTING A KILLER

Harold "Hank" Wilson was sitting on his horse looking out across the small valley where some of his cattle were grazing peacefully. His whole purpose for being there was to check on his cattle to make sure they were doing well. He was not there expecting trouble.

It wasn't until he looked off to the east that he saw the horse Billy had taken early in the morning that he realized there was something wrong. Billy was a young ranch hand who had been working for him for about a year. He had taken the horse to ride out and keep an eye on the cattle, and protect them from varmints. The horse was standing in the pasture grazing peacefully, but there was no sign of Billy.

Hank nudged his horse toward the horse Billy had been riding that morning. The horse raised its head as he rode closer. The horse obviously recognized the horse and rider approaching and did not try to run away or even back away. When Hank rode up alongside the horse, he reached out and took hold of the reins. He noticed there was blood on the saddle. Hank immediately became concerned and began looking around for Billy, but he didn't see him.

Not finding Billy right away, Hank looked at the tracks made by Billy's horse. He quickly began to backtrack the horse. He hadn't gone very far when he saw Billy lying in a shallow ravine. Billy was lying face down on the ground only a few yards from a watering hole. Hank jumped down off his horse and ran to Billy in the hope of helping him. The first thing Hank noticed was that Billy had been shot in the back. He rolled Billy over to see if he could help him, but there was nothing he could do. Billy was dead.

Hank looked around but didn't see anyone. He got Billy's bedroll off his saddle and wrapped him up in it. As soon as he had Billy lying over his saddle, Hank took him back to the ranch house. When he arrived at the ranch house, he tied the horses to the hitching rail in front, then went inside. He walked into the kitchen where he found "Cookie".

"Cookie, I want you to ring the dinner bell. Ring it long and loud."

"It ain't dinner time, yet, boss."

"Ring it anyway. I want as many ranch hands here as soon as possible."

"Okay," Cookie said realizing there was something wrong.

Cookie stepped out on the back porch of the ranch house and began ringing the dinner bell. He rang it hard and long to let the others know there was something wrong.

It wasn't long and the ranch hands started coming toward the ranch house, most of them running. A couple of them came from around in front of the ranch house and had a pretty good idea why the dinner bell had been rung.

Hank stood on the back porch and watched as the ranch hands gathered around. Those who arrived first were talking among themselves while waiting for the rest. It took a minute or so for Hank to quiet the ranch hands down.

"I called you all here because I found Billy over in the east pasture with a bullet hole in his back. Someone shot him in cold blood," Hank said with anger in his voice.

The ranch hands began talking among themselves again. It was clear that they liked Billy. Hank could hear the anger in their voices. They were ready to go after the person who had killed Billy, but they had no idea who shot him.

"Quiet. I need you to listen," Hank said then waited until they had calmed down and were ready to listen to him.

"Okay. Does anyone here have any idea who might have hated Billy enough to kill him?"

The ranch hands just looked at each other and shook their heads, but didn't say anything. They all knew that Billy was an easy-going kind of young man.

"Do any of you know if Billy had a fight, or maybe a verbal disagreement with someone lately?"

"There was this one guy in the saloon in town that didn't like Billy talking to one of the gals who works in the saloon. Billy didn't get angry about it. He just walked away and finished his drink at the bar," Josh Kindry said, one of the old timers.

"What did the guy do?"

"He sat down at the table with the girl. That was all there was to it."

"Anyone else see or hear anything?" Hank asked as he looked at the men.

"I saw it, too. The guy seemed upset over the girl talking to Billy, but when Billy walked away without giving the guy a hard time, he sat down at a table with the girl," Andy said.

"Did Billy say anything about it?"

"No. He just shrugged his shoulders and finished his drink. Shortly after that we all left the saloon and rode back here."

"Did you all ride back together?"

"Yeah," Andy said.

"When did this happen?"

"Last Saturday night, after payday," Josh said.

"Okay. Josh, you and Andy take care of Billy. Owen and Smithy, get saddled up. You will be going with me. Saddle me a fresh horse."

Josh and Andy went around to the front of the ranch house and got Billy. They took him up on the hill where they buried him. Josh said a few words from the Good Book before they returned to the ranch house.

Owen and Smithy, saddled horses, got their rifles and then went up to the ranch house. They had just arrived at the ranch house when Hank came out. He slid his rifle in the saddle scabbard then swung into the saddle.

The three of them rode out the gate and headed toward the east pasture. It didn't take them very long to get to the place where Hank had found Billy. Owen and Smithy stayed on their horses while Hank stepped out of the saddle. He handed Smithy the reins to his horse then began to look around. Hank studied the ground around the area where he found Billy. He was looking for tracks that might tell him where the shooter had been when he shot Billy.

The first thing Hank found were the tracks from Billy's horse. He turned and looked at his two ranch hands while they waited for him. He could see that they were looking around as if they might be expecting trouble.

"I'm not sure that Billy was shot here where I found him. We're going to backtrack his horse."

Hank returned to his horse and swung into the saddle. He gently nudged his horse and began following the tracks left by Billy's horse. They hadn't gone very far when they came upon a place where the ground had been torn up a bit. Hank stepped out of the saddle to study it. It was clear that a horse had suddenly swung around and took off at a run. It was obvious that it had been Billy's horse.

"It looks like this is the place where Billy was shot. His horse swung around and took off. I would say that Billy must have been able to hang onto the horse for at least a little while since I found him over two hundred yards from here," Hank said as he continued to study the tracks.

"Have you figured out where he was shot from?" Owen asked.

Hank stood up and looked toward a row of trees along the edge of a shallow ravine. From the look of the tracks, he guessed that Billy saw the shooter, then quickly wheeled his horse around before he was shot. For Billy to do that, he must have seen that the shooter already had him in his sights.

"The shooter probably shot from those trees. Billy was trying to get away when he was shot."

Owen and Smithy looked toward the trees. They were looking for anyone who might be in the wooded area.

"Stay here and keep an eye out," Hank said as he handed the reins of his horse to Smithy.

Hank drew his pistol from his holster and began walking slowly toward the trees. As he approached the wooded area, he slowed and looked down. He couldn't see anything unusual. He looked up and stepped into the wooded area. Hank walked along the edge of the wooded area until he came upon a place where the ground at the base of a tree had been disturbed. He knelt down and discovered two cartridge casings from 44-40 bullets. Hank knew that a 44-40 caliber rifle was not all that common in the area. He picked up the cartridge casings and put them in his pocket.

He looked toward where Owen and Smithy were sitting on their horses. Hank could see that it would be an easy shot from where he was to where his men were sitting on their horses.

He began walking back and forth in the area. With each time, he moved deeper into the wooded area. Hank had not gone more than thirty feet when he came out of the wooded area to a shallow creek. He looked over the area and found the tracks of a horse and footprints from cowboy boots in the dirt at the edge of the creek.

Hank squatted down and studied the tracks from the horse and from the cowboy boots. He noticed that the boot print in the dirt showed the heel of the left boot was worn hard on the outer edge and had a nail missing. The horse had a right front horseshoe that left a distinct print in the dirt due to a nick in it on the inside back edge of the horseshoe.

With what Hank had found, it would be fairly easy to identify the shooter, if they could find him. He stood up and looked out across the prairie. He wondered where the shooter might have gone, and why he was there in the first place. He knew that the closest town was in the opposite direction from the direction that the horse had come into the wooded area, but he could have made a wide swing around to avoid being seen in the area. He also wondered if the shooter was the same man Billy had apparently offended in town by talking to the girl in the saloon. Hank turned and looked back at the wooded area for a minute then started back to where his ranch hands were waiting for him.

When he came out of the wooded area, he saw Owen had gotten off his horse and was looking at something on the ground. Hank saw Owen bend down and pick it up. He walked up to Owen and looked at his hands.

"What have you got there?" Hank asked.

"I'm not sure. It looks like a silver button," Owen said as he looked at Hank.

Owen handed it to Hank and watched as he looked at it.

"It is a silver button, but where did it come from?"

"I found it right here," Owen said as he pointed at the ground near his feet.

"I know where you found it. What I want to know is where it came from. Do you know anyone who has a shirt, jacket or possibly a vest with silver buttons on it like this one?"

"No, I don't think so," Owen said thoughtfully.

"Do you know anyone who has a shirt or jacket with silver buttons on it?" Hank asked Smithy.

"No, sir."

"It's clean, so it hasn't been here very long," Hank said. "I'm going to keep it for a while. I'll give it back to you, if we find out it has nothing to do with Billy's death."

"That's fine. I don't have any use for it anyway," Owen said.

"What do we do now, boss?" Smithy asked.

"I think it would be a good idea if we go into town. I would like to see if anyone might know who this button belongs to. I also would like to know who might own a 44-40 caliber rifle."

Hank took the reins of his horse from Smithy, swung into the saddle. The three of them headed for town.

As the three rode into town and were headed down the street, Smithy reached over and touched Hank on the arm. When Hank looked at him, Smithy pointed to a black and white paint tied to the hitching rail in front of the Purple Garter Saloon. Hank looked back at Smithy with a look on his face indicating he didn't understand the importance of the horse, but nothing was said for now.

They rode down the street a little further then pulled up in front of the mercantile store. They stepped out of their saddles and tied the reins of their horses to the hitching rail. Hank looked around before he motioned for Smithy to come closer. Both Smithy and Owen moved up close to Hank.

"I saw the horse you pointed out. What about it?" Hank asked.

"That horse belongs to the guy who didn't like Billy talking to the girl in the saloon. At least that's the horse I'd seen him ridin'," Smithy said.

"Are you sure?"

"Yeah, I'm sure."

"The horse looks like it might have traveled some distance and in a hurry," Owen added.

Hank began to think about what his two ranch hands said. He turned and looked down the street toward the horse. His mind was working hard to figure out what was going on and what he should do next.

"I think we should go over to the saloon and have us a drink," Hank finally said.

Smithy and Owen looked at each other and began to grin.

"We're with ya, boss," Smithy said.

"Owen, I want you to go into the mercantile store and leave out the back so no one sees you. You are to cover us from the back of the saloon. We'll give you time to get there. Smithy, you come with me."

As soon as Owen went into the mercantile store, Smithy and Hank drew their pistols and checked them to make sure they were ready to use. Ready for whatever might happen, they started walking toward the saloon on the boardwalk. When they arrived at the front of the saloon, they stopped. Hank stepped off the boardwalk and walked up to the black and white paint. He reached up and gently patted the horse on the neck.

The first thing he noticed was the horse was damp indicating it had been ridden recently and may have been ridden hard. Hank ran his hand down the horse's chest and on down to his right front leg. He lifted the horse's leg and looked at the horseshoe. It had a nick on the inside back edge. There was also dark dirt on the horse's hoof like that on the bank of the creek.

Just as Hank let go of the horse's leg and gently patted it on the neck, he heard the saloon doors open. He turned and looked toward the saloon door. A tall, well-built man dressed in black and wearing a gun tied down on his leg stepped out of the saloon.

"What do you think you're doing with my horse?" the man said with a bit of anger in his voice.

"I was just admiring the animal. We don't see too many horses like this one around here," Hank said with a smile. "It's a shame that a horse like this has to stand out here all wet. Anyone should know that the horse needs to be rubbed down after a hard ride."

"What I do with my horse is none of your business," he said sharply.

"Okay," Hank said then turned and looked at Smithy. "What do you say to havin' a drink?"

"Sure enough."

Smithy and Hank walked past the man and went into the saloon. Once inside, they walked up to the bar and ordered beers. As soon as they had their beers, they walked across the room and sat down at a table close to the wall.

They had been sitting at the table for a little while when the man in black came back into the saloon. He walked up to the bar, ordered a beer, then just stood at the bar watching Smithy and Hank in the mirror behind the bar.

It was clear to Hank that they were being watched. Hank was sort of studying the man in black. As he looked at his boots, he noticed that the heel of his left boot was worn hard on the outside edge. When the man walked into the bar, Hank had also noticed that he had a slight limp which might have contributed to the condition of the heel of his left boot.

Smithy leaned over to Hank and lightly tapped him on the arm. Hank looked at Smithy wondering what was on his mind.

"When we turned to come inside, I saw what looked like a 44-40 caliber saddle rifle in the saddle scabbard on that paint. There was also what looked like a silver button on the scabbard," Smithy whispered. "I couldn't see if there was one of them buttons missin'."

"I think that's the guy we're looking for. His horse's right front shoe has a nick in it that matches the hoof print I found at the creek. His boot heel also matches a boot print at the creek."

"What do we do now?" Smithy asked.

Hank didn't have a chance to answer. Out of the corner of his eye he saw the man start to turn around. He was reaching for his gun as he turned. Hank pushed Smithy over as he dove for the floor. A shot rang out as the two of them dropped to the floor.

Hank quickly drew his gun as he rolled over. He got a quick shot at the man, but missed him. The man darted out the front door of the saloon. The man fired another shot at Hank as he ran out the door, but it went wild hitting a lamp on the wall.

Hank jumped up just as Owen came in the backdoor of the saloon. He glanced at Smithy and noticed there was blood on his shirt sleeve.

"Take care of him," Hank said to Owen as he headed for the door.

When Hank got to the door of the saloon, he hesitated for a second. He didn't want to run out only to find the man waiting for him. Hank peeked around the edge of the door just in time to see the man run around the corner of the mercantile store.

Keeping an eye on the place where the man disappeared around the corner, Hank gave chase. When he got to the corner of the store, he stopped and peeked around the corner. He spotted the man just in time to duck back around the corner. The man fired another shot at Hank. The shot missed Hank but hit the side of the store.

Hank again peeked around the corner of the store. He didn't see the man. He took off after him, again checking before running around the corner of another building.

Once past the second building, there was nothing but open space all the way to the livery stable. Hank caught a glimpse of the man as he ran into the stable. He followed him and ducked behind several bales of hay in front of the livery stable. As far as he knew there were no doors or windows in the back of the stable, only on the one side where a small corral was located. There were only three horses in the corral.

From where Hank was located he could see the corral and the door leading to it, and the front of the livery stable. He waited to see what was going to happen, but there was not a sound from inside the stable. Hank grew impatient. It was beginning to look like he was going to have to go in and get him.

"There's no place for you to go. We have the livery stable surrounded," Hank called out.

Hank didn't get a reply. He was beginning to think that the man had gotten out of the livery stable somehow. Hank had wondered if the man had ducked out, but he had been able to see the side with the door and the front of the livery stable from the time the man entered the livery stable.

It suddenly dawned on Hank. There was a way out of the livery stable that he could not see from his position. It was a long drop to the ground from the rear hay loft door, but it was possible for him to make it. There were also a number of ropes in the livery stable he could use to lower himself to the ground if he didn't think he could make the jump down.

Hank saw Owen running toward him. He waited until Owen knelt down next to him.

"Keep an eye on the front and side. I'm going around to the back."

Hank stood up and ran hunched over around the small corral. When he got to the back corner of the corral, he knelt down at the corner post. He could see that the loft door was open. Hank looked around in the hope of seeing something that would tell him where the man had gone.

As Hank stood at the corner of the corral to think, he wondered if the man had actually gotten out of the livery stable by using the loft door. He looked around at what was close by in the hope of seeing the man if he had gotten out of the livery stable.

About fifty yards from the back of the livery stable was a creek with rather thick trees and brushes along both sides of it. There were only a couple of places where the water in the creek could be seen, and a few places where a man could hide without being seen.

The fifty yards between the livery stable and the trees was wide open. There was very little cover, making it difficult to get to the trees without being an easy target. There was also the thought that the man was still in the livery stable, making it easy to shoot at anyone moving from the livery stable to the trees.

Hank waited at the corner of the corral and watched for any movement in the trees along the creek. Nothing moved, not so much as a leaf. It was deadly quiet. There was not a sound, not even the rustling of a leaf. Hank was slowly growing impatient.

As he waited, he thought about the situation. To run across the open space toward the creek would make him a target from the trees and from the livery stable. That thought left him only one clear possibility that made any sense, and that was to make sure he was not in the barn. Hank ran back to where Owen was waiting and watching the front of the livery stable.

"Keep me covered. I'm going into the barn," Hank said.

Owen nodded that he understood.

Hank took off at a run. He ran up next to the front door of the livery stable and leaned against the wall. He took a couple of deep breaths, then, gripping his pistol in his hand, he ran into the livery stable and dove into a stall near the door. A shot rang out from the loft above him, but the slug hit one of the heavy boards that made up the side of the stall.

"There's no way out of here," Hank called out to the man, but got no response.

Hank just listened. He could hear him moving around in the loft. He could also see dust trickle down between the boards in the loft floor. That gave Hank a good idea where the man was. When the dust was trickling down in the stall next to the one Hank was in, he stood up and fired five rounds up into the floor boards of the loft.

Hank heard a man scream in pain, and thought he heard a body fall, but it didn't sound like it fell on the floor. While watching the floor of the loft, he quickly reloaded his gun. Still watching and listening for any movement, Hank saw several drops of blood slowly drip down from between the boards.

After several more minutes had passed, Hank moved out of the stall and looked up at the loft. With his gun pointed up at the loft, he slowly moved to the ladder. Cautiously, he climbed the ladder until he could see into the loft. The man he had been chasing was lying across a bale of hay, his gun lying off to the side. Hank climbed into the loft and walked over to the man. He was dead.

Hank climbed down and walked out of the livery stable. Owen stood up and followed Hank back toward the saloon. They walked into the saloon and up to the bar. The barkeep poured them a beer and waited for them to take a drink. Hank spoke first.

"Do you know who the man was who rode that paint out front?"

"Yeah. He's William Turner," the barkeep said.

"I never heard of him. Why did he kill Billy?"

"Don't know, but if what I've heard is true, he would kill anyone he didn't like. He didn't like Billy talking to the girl a few days back."

"It don't make no sense," Owen said.

"You're right. Murder seldom does. Let's get Smithy and head back to the ranch. We're done here."

Hank and Owen finished their beers, went to the doc's office and got Smithy. Hank told the doc about the body in the livery stable. Since doc was also the undertaker, he said he would take care of it.

Hank and his ranch hands left the doctor's office. They mounted up and rode back to the ranch. The ranch hands would miss Billy, but life would go on.

ALONE ON THE PRAIRIE

The day was clear and the sun shone down on the vast prairie. Off to the west, the dark green of the forest miles away made the distant hills look black. A gentle breeze caused the tall grasses of the prairie to move back and forth like the waves of an ocean, only green. Off in the distance a small herd of antelope could be seen enjoying the peaceful afternoon.

A covered wagon drawn by four large mules slowly moved west along a trail through the grass. A man walked alongside the wagon, talking to the mules and keeping them pointed toward the Black Hills. On the seat of the wagon was a woman with a young boy sitting beside her. Richard Walker, his wife, Loraine, and their eight-year-old son, Josh, had been traveling for several months. It had been a long time since they had seen another human being, but that was soon to change.

Suddenly, out of a ravine, off to the north, came seven Indians. They were riding hard toward the wagon and yelling at the top of their voices. The look on their faces was not a look one would think of as friendly.

"Get down in the wagon," Richard shouted. "Grab the shotgun and wait until they get close before you fire."

Richard pulled the mules to a stop, then tied the reins to the wagon. He grabbed his rifle from the wagon and took cover near the back of the wagon. He took careful aim at the Indian who was leading the rest of the Indians toward them. He aimed carefully in an effort to make every shot count. He slowly pulled the trigger. When the gun fired, the lead Indian went flying off his horse. Richard fired three more shots before the Indians were close enough to make a pistol useful. He drew his pistol and fired a couple of more shots. Another Indian went down.

The sudden sound of the shotgun firing and seeing two horses and their riders fall to the ground, assured Richard that his wife had done what he had told her to do. The remaining three Indians quickly turned their horses and retreated until they were well out of range of both the shotgun and the rifle. Their attack on the wagon had failed.

Richard stood up and moved along the side of the wagon, then lifted the canvas and looked inside. His son was sitting next to his mother and still had a couple of shotgun shells in his hands ready to hand her. He could see Loraine still had the shotgun sticking out the other side of the wagon. She was watching the three Indians who had ridden away, but had pulled up and were sitting on their horses while looking toward the wagon.

"You did well," Richard said.

"What are they doing?" she asked.

Richard stepped to the back of the wagon and looked toward the Indians. Two horses were standing close to their rides. One was limping while the other one just stood there with its head hanging down. One of the Indians who had taken some buckshot from the shotgun was sitting up with his hands over his face. Richard could not see the other one.

"I'm not sure, but it would be my guess they are waiting to see what we are going to do."

"What are we going to do?" she asked.

"We are going to move away from here so they can come and get their injured friends and horses."

"Do you think that is a good idea?"

"Yes. If we move away so they can tend to their wounded friends, they may decide to leave us alone," Richard said. "We have shown them that we are not afraid of them. We have also showed them that we are good fighters. I'm told that Indians respect good fighters."

Loraine looked at Richard for a moment then smiled at him.

"I'm glad they didn't get close enough to see my face. If they had, they would know just how afraid of them I am," Loraine said looking a little embarrassed.

"It's okay to be frightened as long as you do what has to be done when it needs to be done. Right now, we have to move on."

Richard set his rifle down while he untied the reins. He picked up his rifle then yelled at the mules to move on. Richard once again walked alongside the wagon but with his rifle in one hand as the mules began pulling the wagon. Loraine stayed in the back of the wagon to keep an eye on the three Indians.

As the wagon moved away from the Indians, the three remaining Indians moved closer to their fallen friends, always staying just out of rifle range. They were not sure if it was a trap to get them to move in closer, or if the pioneers were moving off so they could tend to the wounded.

Loraine could see the Indians stop and check on their friends. She could see that two of the ones she had shot at were able to sit up. As they moved out of sight of the Indians, she had a feeling of relief come over her. At least, the Indians had not come after them.

The afternoon proved to be very quiet. Both Loraine and Richard kept an eye out for any danger that might befall them. They were also deep in thought.

Nothing had been said as they continued to move slowly across the prairie. As the sun was about to drop over the horizon, they came upon a shallow river. On the far side of the river were a number of large cottonwood trees. Richard pulled the reins on the mules and yelled for them to stop. He stood looking at the river and the other side.

"I think we should cross the river now," Richard said as he turned to look at Loraine. "There is better cover and more wood for a fire on the other side."

"Is it safe to cross here?" Loraine asked.

"It looks good, but I think I'll wade out and see if it is safe," Richard said as he tied the reins to the wagon.

Richard stepped out into the river. He found that it was no more than about six to ten inches deep all the way across. He turned around and started back toward the wagon. As he waded out of the river, he looked back along the route they had used. He thought he could see something move. He wasn't sure what it was; but if he had to guess, it was the Indians they had the skirmish with several miles back. Richard continued to look, but didn't see any more movement.

"What is it?" Loraine asked.

"I thought I saw something back there," he said then looked up at her. "We need to get to the other side of the river before it gets dark."

Richard climbed up on the seat of the wagon, picked up the reins then yelled at the mules to move on. The mules took up the slack in the harness and began pulling the wagon. The mules pulled the wagon into the river then on across to the other side. It took a bit of effort on the part of the mules to pull the wagon up out of the river and onto the river bank, but they did their job well.

Once on level ground, Richard pulled the mules to a stop. He took a minute to look up and down the river. He was looking for a good place to set up for the night.

"I think we should go up river a little ways. That small grove of trees looks like a good place to spend the night," he said as he pointed at the trees.

"That does look like a nice place," Loraine said with a grin.

Richard turned the mules and started north just a short way off the bank of the river. It wasn't long and they were at the edge of the grove of trees. While Richard was positioning the wagon where he wanted it, Josh was collecting wood for a fire.

As soon as the camp was set up, Loraine prepared dinner for them. Richard took the mules to the river for a drink. When they were done, he hobbled them where they could eat the thick grass.

After dinner, Richard brought the mules in close to the wagon. He tied them to the side of the wagon opposite the fire. He sat next to a tree and listened to the sounds of the night. It would take him a while to learn what sounds were normal and what sounds were not.

"What are you thinking, Richard?" Loraine asked.

"I'm just listening to the night."

"Did you see something back there?"

"I'm not sure. I thought I saw some movement behind us. It seemed to be following the trail we left in the grass."

"Do you think it might be the Indians?"

"It could have been, but I'm not sure."

"Who else could it be out here?" she asked.

"I don't know. We hurt the Indians pretty bad. We killed at least one, possibly two, of them, and left at least two of them injured. I can't see them leaving the injured ones to take care of themselves while they come after us."

"But they don't think like us," Loraine said.

"That may be true, but they know we are well armed and are not afraid to fight them. They also know that we were willing to move on so they can care for the injured. Besides, that was just a hunting party. They were not out to attack us. We just happened to be there. We probably looked like an easy target."

"Okay, let's say you are right. If you are, then who did you see?"

"I don't know," Richard admitted. "It could have been a couple of animals I saw, but we will take precautions tonight."

"What do we do?"

"We let the fire go down to coals. When that happens, I will climb up in that big tree over there," Richard said as he casually pointed in the general direction. "I will keep watch from there."

"What about me."

"You will stay in the wagon and keep a pistol and the shotgun handy. Josh will sleep under the wagon seat out of the way."

"Okay. What do we do now?"

"It's pretty dark. You and Josh climb into the wagon as if you are going to sleep. I'll sit up until the fire burns down."

"Okay. Goodnight, Richard," Loraine said.

She stood up, then leaned down and kissed Richard goodnight.

"Goodnight, Honey."

"Josh, time for bed," Loraine said.

"Goodnight, Daddy."

"Goodnight, Josh," Richard said then gave his son a kiss.

Richard could hear them as they settled into bed. It wasn't long and it was quiet again. He waited in the quiet of the night for the fire to burn down to coals. As soon as it was dark enough that he could not see anything more than about fifteen to twenty feet away, he grabbed his rifle and walked over to the large cottonwood tree. Being as quiet as possible, Richard carefully climbed up into the tree. He made himself as comfortable as possible in the tree. He was about twelve feet above the ground and well hidden in among the branches and leaves.

Richard had been in the tree for over an hour when he heard the sound of a large bird landing just a few branches away from him. It was an owl. For what seemed like a long time, the two of them just looked at each other. Richard even thought about talking to the bird, but thought better of it. Talking to the bird might give away his position if someone was close.

All of a sudden, the big bird turned, looked down toward the river, then flew away. Richard had heard nothing, but the bird apparently had heard something. Richard looked toward the river and listened carefully.

The river flowed by their camp at a rather slow rate, not making a sound. Suddenly, there was the sound of water as if something had caused a ripple in the water. He heard another and another. Someone was riding a horse into the river directly across from their camp.

Richard waited and watched. He thought it was probably the three Indians left after their attack on him and his family. That was until he heard the sound of the clicking of a horseshoe on a rock as the horse stepped out of the river. The horseshoe clicking on a rock meant that whoever was sneaking up on their camp was probably a white man.

"It's just like them greenhorns ta not leave someone watchin'," a voice said in a whisper.

Richard could see them as they stepped out of the saddle and tied their horses to a tree only ten feet or so from the tree he was in.

"Yeah," a second voice whispered. "I'll bet they've got plenty of things in that wagon we could sell at the tradin' post up north. The wagon would bring a bit, too."

"Yeah, and that woman would fetch a pretty price from them Injuns back a ways."

Richard quickly realized that the two men were there to do them harm. He was not about to let that happen. He could clearly see the outline of one of the men. The man was moving toward the wagon. The other man he lost track of for a moment.

"That's far enough. One more move and you will be dead," Richard said.

They turned and looked toward the tree, but could not see anyone at the base of the tree. The man drew his gun and fired a shot at the tree. It was quickly followed by the sound of a rifle being fired.

The slug from the rifle hit the man square in the chest sending him backward onto his back. The other man ducked down by the wagon.

"You picked the wrong place to hide," Richard said from up in the tree. "You can't hide from me."

The sound of Richard's voice scared the man. He was sure it came from the tree, but he could not see anyone. It was as if it was a ghost talking to him.

"Toss your gun out and step away from the wagon with your hands in the air, or die."

He looked first at the wagon, then toward the horses. He thought about making a run for his horse, but his friend's body was lying between him and the horses.

"Time is running out. Lay face down on the ground, or die where you stand."

The man looked around, but he still saw no one. Sweat began to run down his face and he was trembling.

"Now!" Richard yelled.

The man dropped to the ground and held his arms out away from his sides.

"Loraine, keep that shotgun on him."

"I have him covered," Loraine said.

Richard climbed down out of the tree. He walked over to the man on the ground and picked up his pistol.

"Get up," Richard ordered the man.

When the man stood up so Richard could see him, he discovered the man was just a kid, not more than sixteen or seventeen years old. Richard got a rope and tied the kid's hands behind is back, then led him to one of the large cottonwood trees.

"Oh, God. Please don't hang me," the kid cried.

"Richard, you're not going to hang him here in front of our son."

"No. I'm not going to hang him in front of our son. I'm just going to secure him to the tree so we can get some sleep. I'll figure out what to do with him in the morning. You can go back to bed."

Loraine let out a sigh of relief. She looked at her husband for a moment then returned to the wagon. Richard tied the kid to the cottonwood tree, then dragged the dead man away from their campsite. He returned and settled down to rest.

When morning came, Loraine stepped out of the wagon. The first thing she saw was Richard building a fire for breakfast. She also saw the kid still tied to the tree. It was easy to see that the kid was afraid of what was going to happen to him. Richard walked up to Loraine and leaned close to her.

"You can fix breakfast for us. We'll feed the kid before we let him go. He has been scared half to death that I'm going to hang him this morning, and I let him think that all night. I don't think he will be causing us, or anyone else, any trouble for a very long time."

"You're going to let him go?"

"Yes. There's no way we can take him with us. We would have to watch him every minute, never knowing what he might do."

"I guess you're right," she said then kissed Richard on the cheek.

Loraine busied herself fixing breakfast. After Richard and his family had eaten their breakfast, he untied the kid. Keeping a gun on him, he allowed the kid to eat. When he was finished eating, Richard tied him up again.

Richard and his family cleaned up their camp and loaded everything back into the wagon. Richard tied one of the two horses to the back of the wagon after hitching up the mules. The other horse, he tied to a tree. As soon as everything was ready, and Loraine and Josh were in the wagon, Richard looked up at Loraine.

"You go on. I'll catch up with you in a little while. I have to take care of the kid. I'll be along shortly."

"Okay," Loraine said then kissed him.

Richard stepped off the wagon, then stood there watching as his wife and son left in the wagon, moving westward. Once they were well on their way, he turned and walked over to the kid.

"It's time," Richard said looking at the kid.

"Oh, God. Please don't hang me," the kid cried as he pleaded.

"I'm not going to hang you. What I am going to do is give you your freedom."

The kid looked at him in disbelief. He could not believe he was going to be let go.

"You're not goin' ta hang me?"

"No. I'm going to let you go. If I see you again, anywhere on this earth, I will kill you on sight."

"I don't believe you."

"You better believe me. I'm going to untie you. You will be free to do whatever you want. Let me make it clear, if you come after me or my family, I will not hesitate to kill you on sight."

"Will I get my horse and my gun back?"

"No. You will get your life back, and that is all. You will have to find your own food, your own place to sleep, and your own way to survive," Richard said, then turned around and walked toward the horse. As he swung up in the saddle, he looked at the kid. The kid was looking at him, there was fear in his eyes.

"You can bury your friend or leave him to the coyotes. I might suggest that you stay close to this river. If nothing else, it could provide you with food in the form of fish."

"You can't do this," he yelled. "I will die out here."

"I not only can, I'm doing it. You are on your own. I'm giving you more of a chance to live than you and your friend would have given me and my family," Richard said then turned the horse around and rode west to join his wife and son. He never once looked back.

Richard Walker and his family arrived in Sturgis just before winter set in. Richard took a job with the city of Sturgis while Loraine became a teacher. Josh grew up and became a soldier stationed at Fort Meade. The Walker family never saw the kid again, and had no idea if he survived.

www.ingramcontent.com/pod-product-compliance
Lightning Source LLC
Chambersburg PA
CBHW071143170626
46809CB00002B/752